*The Greatest Team to
Ever Step onto the Hardwood in the
Basketball-Rich State of Kentucky*

David L. Sullender

Archway Publishing books may be ordered
through booksellers or by contacting:

Archway Publishing
1663 Liberty Drive
Bloomington, IN 47403
www.archwaypublishing.com
1-(888)-242-5904

Because of the dynamic nature of the Internet, any web addresses or
links contained in this book may have changed since publication and
may no longer be valid. The views expressed in this work are solely those
of the author and do not necessarily reflect the views of the publisher,
and the publisher hereby disclaims any responsibility for them.

Any people depicted in stock imagery provided by Thinkstock are
models, and such images are being used for illustrative purposes only.
Certain stock imagery © Thinkstock.

ISBN: 978-1-4808-0359-6 (sc)
ISBN: 978-1-4808-0361-9 (hc)
ISBN: 978-1-4808-0360-2 (e)

Library of Congress Control Number: 2013920382

Printed in the United States of America

Archway Publishing rev. date: 11/14/2013

Thank you, RJ Rigsby—practice more!

"If a coach is determined to stay in the coaching profession, he will develop from year to year. This much is true, no coach has a monopoly on the knowledge of basketball. There are no secrets in the game. The only secrets, if there are any, are good teaching of sound fundamentals, intelligent handling of men, a sound system of play, and the ability to instill in the boys a desire to win."

—Adolph Rupp

Introduction

THERE I WAS, THE SKINNY little white boy sporting the new Converse high tops and the green-and-gold knee-high socks that, believe it or not, were the fashion in the early eighties. I was guarding our opponent's (Holy Church) point guard, who was dribbling the ball up the floor toward their basket. As I forced the guard toward the sideline, I positioned myself to intercept any pass he might attempt, and he did just that. I took off like a rocket toward the ball, intercepted his pass, and then ran the length of the floor for an uncontested layup. Their coach called a time-out. It was pure pandemonium! The gym went crazy with our fans yelling from their seats, and our bench players and coaches loudly and enthusiastically congratulating our hard play as the opposing coach screamed at his players for their sloppy effort.

It wasn't a typical Friday night basketball game with the smell of wood, sweat, and leather that players came to love. We had just taken the lead on the best team in our region. No one ever imagined that we could even play with this team, let alone beat them. And here we were with two minutes left in the game, poised to do just that. This was going to be the biggest upset of our 1984 basketball season. The officials ended the time-out, instructed the players back to the floor, and handed Holy Church the ball, and the game resumed. That is when it all fell apart.

I never saw the guard rush past me, but I swear I could see the flames coming off his shoes as he drove to the basket as if I wasn't even there. They scored. The lead seesawed back and forth for the next minute or so. Holy Church then decided to foul us every time we touched the ball. Their coach wanted to put us on the foul line and test our ability to shoot free throws for the remainder of the game. He was betting that we would miss them, allowing his team a chance to get the ball and score. He was correct.

We missed shot after shot as they scored basket after basket. I must have gone to the foul line four times in the final minute, only to see my shots sail off to the left or right. And just like that my hopes, dreams, and visions (as well as my basketball career) sailed away as the final buzzer blared, dashing any prospect of a huge upset. Holy Church won the game.

Like most kids growing up in the state of Kentucky, basketball was the king sport and the one sports season that I truly looked forward to year after year. Everyone plays the game in this state. You can always find a pickup game at most schools, churches, playgrounds, or just about anywhere with a ball and a basket to shoot it in. If we weren't playing the game, we were watching it on television or listening to it on the radio or talking about it in our groups. Basketball is the rite of passage in Kentucky, and when the season began, nothing else was planned for those two game nights each week.

So losing to Holy Church when we had the game all but won was another shot in the stomach of what was a very long and unsuccessful season. We really thought we would be unbeatable that year with five experienced players returning for their senior season. We were wrong. We only won four games the entire season—undoubtedly one of the worst basketball teams to play in our school's history. It was embarrassing, sickening, disheartening, and exhausting week after week to lose to opponent after opponent. The worst part of that season was walking off the floor after yet another defeat and catching the eyes of those who'd worn the uniform seasons before us. You could see the confused and angry disbelief in their eyes as we exited the floor toward the locker room.

Even worse was seeing my twin brother, Don, exiting the stands disappointed as always in our efforts on the floor. That was probably the hardest part of losing for me because I often needed his support and approval, especially in basketball. We were surviving our parents' divorce, which consisted of a stepfather who never really cared about us anyway and a mother who was absent for most of my senior year, leaving my twin and me to care for our younger brother Kenny. Understandably so, those games then became life itself for me and my brother. He and my uncle would often attend the games to support me. Interestingly, I always felt that my twin was a much better player than I, but he had just lost interest after his junior year. Even to this day, some thirty years later, he still has one of the purest, fundamentally perfect, and pretty shots I have ever seen on any player. His form was perfect with his shooting arm extended and his hand pointing to the basket, often resulting in two points. He was such a good player and competitor that another loss for me was another loss for him as well.

So not only was the defeat in our season-ending tournament the proverbial final nail in the coffin, it was also the end of my career in basketball as I had come to know it. There was no way I could have known that the experience of my senior year of basketball and life afterward would help prepare me for meeting and playing with the Great Eight and one of the best teams to ever play in Kentucky.

You see, greatness comes in many forms and fashions these days, and people are often considered "great" too easily, in my opinion. Then again, not many people have experienced greatness as I have. So when I witnessed something great (and, no, I'm not talking about NCAA-championship or high-school-state-title great) that was the result of hard work, dedication, respect, trust, and love, I was compelled to write this book. Not only to share the experience but to pay tribute to those young men who gave me one of the greatest treasures of my life. It came in the form of 27.5, 8.6, 4, and 8.

In writing this book I pay tribute to those eight young men who afforded me one of the greatest experiences of my life. Yes, those eight young souls and that first season became the inspiration for writing this book. They became the Great Eight and the greatest team to ever step onto the hardwood in the basketball-rich state of Kentucky.

CHAPTER 1

My History

AFTER MY SENIOR YEAR IN high school, like many kids, I went to college, then joined the army, and ended up back in my hometown. I managed to continue improving my basketball skills by playing in various city leagues, but nothing was quite as fun as playing for our high school team. I really missed suiting up to take the floor representing our school and community. However, I have never stepped onto our high school basketball court since our season ended in 1984.

I have never seen another game in that gym since playing there my senior year. After such a disappointing season, I needed some time away from both the school and the sport. And after quite a while without contacting anyone from our team, it was too late and unnecessary to go back.

So my thirty-year journey, which would eventually lead me back home, began. It was a couple of years after school that my mother moved to Nashville, Tennessee. Bored with the area that I grew up in and the same routine day after day, I decided to join her and move to Nashville as well.

Nashville was a great place to live. Besides the obvious music scene, career opportunities, and affordable living, I found that there were lots of basketball courts for pickup games and many gyms offering various leagues in which to play. I soon settled into this new town and joined a gym, which offered basketball in a city league. It wasn't long before I was on a team and playing ball against other teams throughout the city. It also wasn't long before I was married and soon after had a beautiful daughter, Meghan. And then, of course, my playing time once again diminished.

Soon, being a husband and father with a career in sales became my new reality. As the years flew by and Meghan started getting older, I began showing her how to play basketball. We worked on her dribbling, shooting, passing, and overall game skills. She actually became quite a little player. I also became aware of something else. I really enjoyed coaching and teaching basketball. I found coaching to be as exciting as actually playing the game. The more I coached and taught her, the more fun it became. As a result of discovering just how much I enjoyed coaching, I began coaching men's basketball in the local YMCA league. This was when my coaching career began, literally due to me passing this wonderful sport on to my daughter. Teaching and developing my daughter's basketball fundamental skills in the driveway pointed me in a direction that would eventually lead me into the path of the greatest players to ever step onto the court in Kentucky.

It's funny how life will prepare you for experiences you encounter as you age. My love of the sport led me to playing in high school, continuing in the military, moving to Nashville, coaching my daughter, and playing and coaching in various city leagues, and then to my main area of interest, coaching.

It began with a call I made to the league director requesting to enter my men's team into their city league. Usually there was a $350 entrance fee required per team. He informed me that the twelve- to fourteen-year-old boys' league was in need of a coach for the upcoming season, and if I would volunteer to coach them, he would waive the $350 registration entrance fee for our men's team. So there it was, an opportunity and excuse to coach and teach boys youth basketball. I accepted his offer, and life as a youth basketball coach began for me.

My first experience coaching a boys' basketball team wasn't the stuff of legend, such as turning teams around and getting a big reputation. It started out pretty much as a bribe.

Although I only coached one season, I knew that coaching was something I would like to return to at some point. At the end of our season, the league changed, along with the director, leaving me without a youth team to coach. So I went back to playing basketball and coaching my own men's team in whichever league we participated.

AFTER A FEW YEARS OF both playing and coaching, my family and career started consuming my time, leaving very little extra time for anything else. The game I came to love was starting to fade further away with the exception of catching a game or two on television with my daughter. One of the advantages of living in Nashville was that I could usually get tickets to see the University of Kentucky play when they came to town to take on Vanderbilt. Trying to get tickets in Lexington was essentially impossible. So between the live games and the TV games, my daughter and I continued to enjoy the Wildcat basketball season.

The years to come were very trying, to say the least. A couple of divorces, a struggling career, a strained business venture, and the loss of both my grandparents, who I fondly remember always in the stands for my games, was starting to burden me more than I thought I could possibly bear. I did not have the time to again get involved with the sport that I had once valued more than anything else. Funny, looking back I can now see that working out on the court would have helped me through some serious difficulties; yet, at that time completely stressed out, I never even considered it.

I will never forget the afternoon I was making a sales call three hours away from home, depressed over my current financial state and the lack of any new business prospects, when I got the phone call.

At the time I was involved in a new business venture that was barely able to pay its bills, creating a financial burden for me that I would never wish on anyone. So the voice on the other end of the line was a nice relief, as if God was finally looking down on me and saying, "You have suffered enough. Here is a chance to get back on track." The voice on the other end of the phone was a human resources manager for a company in Kentucky looking for a sales manager. I was invited to a meeting with their director of sales, who would interview me for the position. This new position would require travel throughout Eastern Kentucky managing nine salespeople, and I would be responsible for growing sales for two branches in the region. This new position and the job requirement were tailor-made for me. I knew I could really do this job. So after a quick meeting with the director of sales and the HR director, I was offered the position, and I was heading back to Kentucky. After twenty-six years living in Nashville, I was finally heading home, except this time I would be residing in Eastern Kentucky, with which I was not familiar but which would eventually facilitate the meeting of the Great Eight.

I quickly packed my bags, loaded up my furniture, gathered my dog and fiancée (who was coincidentally from the town to which I was relocating), and headed northeast toward Eastern Kentucky. My daughter, who was attending college in Nashville at that time, elected to remain there with her mother. Kentucky is the home of coal mining, the land of college basketball, the capital of bourbon, and the home of the greatest team to ever step onto the hardwood of this basketball-rich state. Somehow, each of those things that Kentucky is known for would eventually touch my life.

CHAPTER 2

Moving to Kentucky

SINCE THIS WAS THE AREA of Kentucky where my fiancée, Tobie grew up, we were able to settle down smoothly and begin this phase of our life together. I was able to step right into my new position and do very well with my responsibilities. We developed new friendships and really started enjoying life again. I still wasn't playing much basketball; however, the new residence allowed me to watch just about every game that the Kentucky Wildcats played, and that excited me. The move also gave us the opportunity to spend a lot of time with my fiancée's family, who I came to know and adore.

I came to appreciate the fact that life in Eastern Kentucky is at a much slower pace than anywhere else I have lived, including the area of Kentucky where I grew up. Eastern Kentucky is quite laid-back, with little stress and no urgency, and the people are mostly very hospitable and kind.

However, poverty is widespread in this region of the state. Since most employment stems from mining coal, its fluctuating market often causes rampant unemployment. This area also seems to be a magnet for those who would take advantage of disability claims. I noticed that many seemed to be able-bodied and could work but chose not to do so. Instead, they live from government check to check, contributing to the state's increasing financial woes and economic downturn. In other words, I had to take the good with the bad in relocating.

My sales team, on the other hand, was doing quite well, working hard and making me look like a sales genius, which really was far from the truth. Because of my experience with sales professionals, I was able to make a quick assessment and determined that as a whole the sales team was very strong. I made a couple of replacements, moved some obstacles from them, and supported their efforts. That formula facilitated my success and that of our sales team. I have come to realize after many years selling for many different sales managers that most managers bring their own style and skill sets to their teams. They require different things; some are micromanagers and want reports on everything, including how many times salespeople stop to use the bathroom. (I actually had a manager who wanted to know this.) Others are hands-off and will only step in when needed. This style of management worked best for me and was the style I adopted with some of my own different requirements. You see, what most managers fail to realize is that salespeople are truly professionals. If they don't sell, they don't earn, and no type or quantity of reports will ever change, enhance, tweak, or replace that fact. The key is hiring the right person. Once that is done, I simply remove all obstacles that get in his or her way, such as a bunch of BS reports. I then genuinely support the salespeople's efforts and needs. Then, with a little adjusting, I watch them grow.

This is not limited to just sales. This is also a successful formula in life as well as in coaching. If you put the right people in the right place, remove their obstacles, and support them, they will succeed. Looking back, I can see that I used the same strategy in coaching that I used in managing my sales team. Again, this was another life lesson that would prepare me later for meeting the Great Eight. Of course, replacing players is next to impossible in most cases, and we typically are stuck with who we inherit, but putting those players we do end up with in the right positions will yield success for any team.

As we settled into our day-to-day lives, we were spending more and more time with Tobie's nephew, Rocky. He was an amazing kid, who was smarter than the typical kid his age. He has a wonderful and funny personality that draws you to him. He is also very quick-witted, which often tickled me. Rocky and I developed a special relationship. We became good friends who enjoyed each other's company whether we were working in the garage on a remodeling project or shooting basketball on a local court. Rocky, however, was much smaller than most kids his age. He was short but stocky with an athletic build. He was excelling in other sports, such as karate, and he loved to play baseball. We attended a few of his games, but due to the difficulties I had sitting through a four-hour baseball game, we only would stay for a few innings.

Then one day we got the news. Rocky was playing basketball for his local school team—finally a sport I could sink me teeth into and enjoy watching him develop in. There was one problem, however. His games were usually Saturday morning. As I mentioned earlier, we were enjoying time with our friends, which meant late Friday nights at our local watering hole. This was not a good formula for rising early on Saturday mornings to attend his basketball games. To say the least, we missed his first few games.

Keep in mind that with all the little twists that life had thrown at me these past few years, I had pretty much forgotten my love of the game. So I wasn't really inclined to toss aside my Friday night activities to attend an early-morning basketball game until Rocky approached me as I was working on one of our projects.

"Uncle Sully, what is your favorite sport?" he asked.

"I would have to say basketball, little buddy," I said. "Why did you ask me that?"

"I was just wondering, since basketball is your favorite sport, why don't you come to any of my games?"

Damn. He just nailed me, I thought. He suckered me into his young web of intellect and caught me speechless.

How do you answer that? The only excuse really that I had for not attending his games was very selfish and pathetic. My excuse of Saturday morning hangovers was not going to satisfy him, and I did not want to explain to him what that meant, so I paused for a minute or two and made Rocky this promise. "I will do everything I can to make the rest of your games this season, little buddy."

I promised, and I intended to do just that.

THE NEXT SATURDAY MORNING WAS game day for Rocky, so we drove down to the gym to watch his game. As I entered the gym in this small Eastern Kentucky town, I started to get those old feelings again churning inside of me that I used to get walking out onto the hardwood. The smell of the gym, the cheers of the fans, cheerleaders, and concessions took me back to the good old days when that leather ball in my hands was a panacea for all problems.

And there he was, on the floor doing his warm-up drills. I noticed he was a little slow with the dribble, couldn't shoot that well, and one more glaring fault. Rocky was the smallest kid on the floor. Immediately my mind kicked into coaching mode. He could play point guard. With his quickness, he could blow by any defense trying to cover him. Then I saw him dribble. Okay, point guard wasn't going to work. If only there was a right fielder's position in basketball.

I thought he might be able to play the No. 2 guard/shooting guard position. If he could work through an off-ball screen, then he could possibly get a good shot. And then I saw him shoot. The only position left that I thought he could do at this point was water boy. Great. I shortened our Friday night fun, woke up early, and drove to the gym to watch him carefully and athletically deliver water to the more talented players. This was going to be a very long morning.

To say the obvious, Rocky did not start. As a matter of fact, I don't remember Rocky getting into the game at all. It really didn't take long to assess the problem. The coach had too many boys on his team. It would have been impossible to teach, instruct, and coach that many kids. Apparently his strategy was to have his best and most talented player run the length of the floor and try to score. The other players just watched and pretty much stayed out of the way. This definitely was going to be a long morning. As unpleasant as watching the chaos was for me, the excitement of being in the gym for a game was starting to return to me. As I sat there watching the circus unfold, I was actually forming strategies and game plans in my head. I was playing the game out in my mind the same way I would coach these boys if I had this team.

The remainder of the season was pretty much like the game we saw: just one guy dribbling toward the basket as the other four watched. The bench players were as tuned out of the game as were most of the parents in the bleachers. There was an obvious void of energy and excitement with this team, and I struggled with the urge to throw myself at the coach with assistance in managing the team. Instead, I would just sit there and observe. This was my introduction to the school's basketball program, and I became acutely aware of one thing: Rocky was going to need a lot of work if he wanted to continue with this sport, and I was going to be the one to teach him. I will say, though, that the hot dogs with sauce and mustard from their concession stand were fantastic. That was the one thing that caused me to hastily make my way to the gym on Saturdays, much to Tobie's displeasure.

"It's not whether you get knocked down; it's whether you get back up."

—Vince Lombardi

CHAPTER 3

Devastating News

It wasn't long after Rocky's basketball season ended that I got back into projects around our home. Tobie had decided to build a fish pond. The problem with that was whenever Tobie decided to build something, it usually meant I had a new project to work on. So before I knew it, we were climbing creek beds in Eastern Kentucky hunting flat river rock for the waterfall that was going to feed the pond. The previous evening we had met some friends that we hadn't seen in a long time, so I was suffering from a headache and dehydration that was surely the result of the evening's activities. As I was gathering rocks and taking them up the huge hill to my truck, my arms ached, and I was short of breath. This continued for the remainder of the day. I had very little energy and was having trouble getting my breath. Upon Tobie's insistence, I made an appointment with my doctor.

Somewhere in rural Eastern Kentucky, on a small partially paved road, a young man pedaled his bicycle lazily through the muggy summer heat. This was his way of wasting a day away when none of his friends were available to hang out with him. He pedaled nowhere in particular, just wherever the road would take him. Mrs. Smith was at her mailbox going through the day's delivery when she saw the young man. She gave him her typical big smile and wave as he pedaled past. Mrs. Smith was very fond of the young man and would often invite him onto the porch for some refreshing lemonade. He pedaled on until he reached the main road and then turned right onto the church parking lot. At the back of the church was a basketball court, and apparently a game was being played. As he approached, he noticed that the boys playing were much older than he, so there would be little chance that he would be invited to participate. Even so, he decided to stay and watch the game. As he stared out across the court, Kyle wondered how this year's basketball season would turn out for him.

At that very moment, across town a young man was wrestling with his neighborhood pals when his mother hollered for him to come inside for the evening. As he walked through the door, she handed him a sheet of paper that was sent home from school for both parents and students to review. The paper was an invitation to try out for the basketball team for the coming school year. Pete's mother asked him if he was interested in playing. A pensive boy told his mother that he would consider it. He had already decided that he would like to play next season, but with a new coach and new boys playing, he wasn't sure if he would still be interested. Pete was a likable and tough kid, and he would need to think more about this.

Neither Kyle nor Pete had any idea that their paths would cross not only on the court but on the team that would become the Great Eight.

Baseball season had recently ended, and that usually meant basketball was just around the corner. Ryan was putting his glove and cleats away when he noticed a team basketball picture hanging on the wall next to his latest baseball photo. "What is this season going to be like?" he wondered. "Will I make the team? Who is going to coach us?" Ryan really loved basketball, and since he was above average in height, it gave him a lot of opportunities for getting picked to play. He had no clue that he would become a very important piece to the puzzle that would make up the Great Eight.

At that exact moment in a different county, a young man was stressed beyond tears. He would be moving to another county at the start of the new school year, which meant meeting new friends and saying good-bye to his lifelong friends. What would the new school be like? Would the new students accept him? Would the new coach like him or think that he was good enough to play? Basketball had become very important to this young man, and he had established himself on his current team as a good scorer. Would it be the same for him at this new school? Reed had no idea that soon he would understand just how valuable he would become to the new team, students, and coaches. Both he and Ryan would soon be joining the team that became the Great Eight.

After a couple of agonizing weeks, I finally made it to my doctor's appointment. My doctor, after examining me, decided to send me to a cardiologist. The cardiologist studied the evaluation results from my primary care doctor and then scheduled a heart catheter procedure for me to determine if there was anything going on in my heart. He assured me that I was probably experiencing some angina or heartburn due to overindulgence the night before.

Everything seemed to go well until at one point during the catheter process, I heard the cardiologist actually say, "Oh no. This is not good." That got my attention, to say the least. He then approached to inform me that I had suffered a heart attack and that I also had an occluded main artery. Normally he would stint the occlusion right there in these situations; however, with my artery being 100 percent closed, he could not risk trying to get a stint in there. That was about as much as I could remember, since I was in a slightly drugged state, dreaming of those hot dogs, no doubt.

The next thing I remember was being wheeled to my recovery room by nurses who were telling me that I was the luckiest man they knew and that I should immediately play the lottery once I left the hospital. Tobie was there waiting for me, looking very concerned. The cardiologist also informed her of my situation, and she did not take the news very well. The news really scared both of us. Later that evening, the cardiologist came to release me and to explain my options. He said that he would not stint me. He also told us that in my situation, smaller arteries had started to form around the clog, allowing me some blood flow. His recommendation was to start medical therapy using a beta-blocker, which would prevent my heart from demanding more blood than my smaller arteries could carry. He wanted to try that for a while and then look at a bypass as an alternative option.

I was very bothered by this because I knew it meant that my activities and projects would have to slow way down. I was just way too young for this. So the medical therapy began, as did some life-changing decisions. This, as I had figured, really sucked.

Not too far away from the hospital, Chad shot his hundredth shot of the day in his family's driveway like he did every morning, playing a game in his head. He was small for his age, but he knew that there were very few boys his age who could outrun him. What he lacked in size he made up in quickness. He kept shooting the ball toward the rim, wondering what the basketball season was going to be like during the coming fall and if he had the stuff to make the team. Just then his shot came up short and to the left. He knew he wouldn't make the team shooting this way, so he started the next hundred shots. Soon in the future, those shots would pay off, as he would find himself playing for one of the greatest teams in Kentucky.

I continued on the beta-blocker for several months, hating every moment of it. The medicine just made me feel bad. I was tired all the time and had very little energy to do anything. My normal weekly chores were taking me twice as long to complete. I tried working out again, but I was lacking the energy for it, so I just quit. This medical therapy option was going to take a lot of time to get used to, and I was running out of patience fast.

While I was contemplating my medical options, across town, sitting on the bench in that warm gym during a weeklong basketball camp, two boys and best friends watched as their team was getting destroyed in front of them. They discussed many things, most of which were not related to basketball. They laughed at the performances, irritating the coach. They both could play as well as most of the boys on the team but were being overlooked at this particular moment. Neither one of them really cared very much as long as they could hang with each other. Wil and Brent were inseparable. They were the best of friends, and both loved the game of basketball. They often wondered how they could get more playing time and contribute more. Little did they know that in a few short months, they would get their wish along with becoming part of the greatest team to ever walk onto the hardwood in the basketball-rich state of Kentucky.

CHAPTER 4

The Great Eight

THE OFF-SEASON WENT BY FAIRLY quickly, and before I knew it, basketball season was right around the corner. Rocky's parents and I had already discussed certain drills that he needed to work on through the summer that would help to improve his game. But, unfortunately, like most kids his age, baseball along with other activities consumed most of his time and interest. So when I approached Rocky one day, I wasn't surprised at how our conversation went.

"Have you been working on the basketball drills I prepared for you last year?" I asked.

"No," was all I got.

"Rocky, how do you expect to get any better without working on your basic basketball skills?"

"You will teach me," he said. As if I could wave the basketball wand over his head and transform him into LeBron James.

"Rocky, we need to start right away on some drills that will make you a better player," I said.

"Okay, Uncle Sully," he replied, flashing me a sheepish grin.

So each week we began working on some basic, simple drills. I showed him dribbling techniques and proper shooting form, and we continued this for several weeks.

I GOT A CALL FROM Rocky's dad (Dustin) one evening. I thought he was going to inform me that Rocky was unable to practice for whatever reason. I was somewhat surprised at what he wanted to discuss with me.

"Sully, you know the basketball season is about to start for Rocky, right?"

"Yes. We have been working pretty hard. He still has a lot to work on, but he is coming along."

"How would you like to help coach the team this year?"

"What ..." was all I could think to say. To actually help coach his team had not even crossed my mind.

"Because of the number of kids interested in playing this year, they are dividing the team up into three different teams. Instead of just one school team playing in the league, we will have three different teams competing against each other and other schools in the league as well.

"We could really use your assistance with the coaches and working with the boys if you are able to free up the time. I have volunteered already myself," he continued.

"Sure," I said. "I would be happy to help out. Just let me know when and where."

"Tomorrow night, at the school," he said. "The entire school's team will practice together for the next couple of practices. Then they will divide them into three different teams."

And just like that, I was drawn into the world of Kentucky basketball, only not as a player; this time I would be coaching. Now here I was, fully entrenched in my own life, which included nights out late with friends dancing and not returning home until the wee hours of the morning. Although we were not doing anything wrong or illegal, it was just that I would need to be sharp around these boys. Currently I was somewhere in between Walter Matthau's character Morris Buttermaker in the movie *Bad News Bears* and Tom Hanks's character Jimmy Dugan from the movie *A League of Their Own*. I smoked cigars and drank quite a bit of beer. Rocky's mother often joked about worrying that she would have to bang on my door the morning of the games just to make sure I was up and ready. That actually could have helped on a few occasions. I definitely needed to clean my life up a little and take it down a notch or two for the next three months. What was I thinking?

The next evening I met up with Rocky and his father and we went to the school for practice. I was a bit nervous because it had been so long since I had coached anyone. Would they accept me? Would they listen to me? Would they play for me? These questions and a million others kept circling in my mind.

As we approached the gym, my nerves were on full alert, and I started to doubt this idea altogether. We proceeded through the front door, down the hallway, and into the gym. And then my mind completely locked up at the sight before me.

Kids were all over the place. There must have been a million of them running around screaming at the tops of their lungs looking like a bunch of wasps swarming around after having their hive struck. They were wrestling on the floor, running in circles, kicking the balls around, and fighting, and some were actually crying, including me. This was it. This was the basketball team that I was to help teach. I was looking for the nearest door. Dustin must have sensed what I was contemplating.

After grabbing my arm to prevent me from sprinting out the door, he led me through the melee toward two adults who were huddling in the corner.

"Sully, these are the other coaches, TJ and Bryan." They looked at me as if a terrorist had just entered their presence. After a quick handshake, they went back to their private conversation. Rocky, his father, and I just stood there patiently waiting for instructions.

After a few minutes, TJ blew the whistle and signaled for all of the players to proceed to the center of the floor. TJ, who was apparently in charge of the basketball teams, instructed the players about the change in the teams for the season and said they would have different coaches this year. They seemed unimpressed. When TJ had finished, Bryan, who was the coach the previous season, broke the players into four groups. He sent two groups to one end of the floor for instruction and drills and then sent the other two groups to the other end of the floor.

He looked at me and smirked. "They're all yours."

Two things were really becoming apparent. First, TJ and Bryan did not seem to like me much, and, second, this was going to be a total waste of my time. After thanking him, Rocky, his father, and I proceeded down to the other end of the floor. Coaching in Kentucky was about to begin.

As I approached the kids, my mind was racing and then jammed up. I could not recall one single drill to have them working on—not one! So I employed old faithful and put them into two lines on each sideline of the court. Then it started to come back to me. *Layup drills.* We began layup drills, which gave me the opportunity to evaluate each kid that came through the line. It also helped me with two other things as well. We were playing with a youth-size ball (27.5 inches), and the height of the goal was eight feet six, neither of which I was remotely familiar with. As practice continued, I was able to remember some other drills for the kids to work on, and then we rotated players to opposite ends of the floor.

Soon practice was over. Dustin and I approached TJ and Bryan, who were once again involved in deep discussions. TJ quickly looked up at me and asked, "Are you willing to take a team and be the head coach this season?"

His words hit me like a ton of bricks. I thought I was just helping out. I was shocked. I thought I was just going to be an assistant or practice coach. I had not considered being a head coach. I simply nodded and nervously said, "Sure, whatever you need me to do."

"Okay. Friday we will divide the teams up into three teams once practice is over. We will determine practice times and team colors then as well. See you guys on Friday. Welcome to Wildcat basketball."

And just like that, I walked into a new school; met a bunch of screaming, panicking, out-of-control kids and two coaches who did not seemed to be impressed with my assistance; and became a head coach for an elementary school team, all of this in a matter of an hour and a half. Welcome to Wildcat basketball indeed.

THE REMAINDER OF THE WEEK flew by, and before I knew it, I was heading back to the gym. It was the night that I would find out what my team would consist of. In the gym parking lot, Rocky and his father approached me.

"Are you ready for tonight?" Dustin asked, smiling from ear to ear.

"Yes, sir, I am definitely ready. As long as I get Rocky on our team, I don't really care who ends up with us. Besides, you know TJ and Bryan are probably taking the best players anyway and leaving us with the scrubs," I said. "I just hope we get some good-enough talent to at least compete."

"I am familiar with most of these kids through baseball, so I can help you pick the players you will want on your team. There is a couple that you definitely do not want on your team."

After of few seconds considering my options, I looked at Rocky's dad and said, "We just need to make sure the other two don't stack their teams, leaving us in bad shape. Once they see who you are requesting, they will know we are watching them and try to get the better players ahead of us."

"Don't worry about that. It will be fine. Let's go."

"On to the gauntlet," I joked.

In the gym we walked toward the other coaches. We were split into two groups again, and practice went about as well as it had the previous time. I did notice the occasional strange looks from both coaches and parents. When practiced ended that night, the two coaches, Rocky's dad, and I met in the middle of the floor. It was time to select our teams.

"I will start, then Bryan, and then you, Sully," TJ said as he handed out the names of the players from which we would choose.

TJ selected his son, who was an exceptional point guard. Bryan followed suit by selecting his son as well, another fantastic point guard.

Now it was my turn. "Who else on this list can play point guard?" I asked.

"Kyle Bentley is a really good player," Dustin said, while the other two remained silent, of course.

"We select Kyle Brentley as our point guard." And that's how it all started. We took our turn choosing the remaining players as I listened to Dustin's advice. When we came across a player who he did not know, I would press both TJ and Bryan for information and would then make my decision.

After choosing Rocky and Kyle, I was able to complete my team. The other two teams ended up with eight and nine players, respectively, but I was only able to get seven players. *It is going to be a lonely bench this year,* I thought. We then decided to choose the colors, and since I had to go last in picking my players, I was able to go first in colors. I chose blue. That meant that our school had a gold team, a white team, and a blue team.

So I finally had my team. The blue team. The Wildcat team. I still had no idea who these players were, nor did I have any idea what I was getting myself into. All I had was a list of names in my hand.

1. Rocky Gaines

2. Kyle Brentley
3. Chad Nelson
4. Ryan Nichols
5. Brian Peterson
6. Wil Payne
7. Pete Self

So now you have met them. Of course, they were still young and raw, but this was our team. The Great Eight. The greatest team to ever take the hardwood in the basketball-rich state of Kentucky. Soon you will understand why even to this very day, I believe this to be true.

CHAPTER 5

The Team

THE TEAM CONSISTED OF A variety of kids with different skill sets. Our team was a potpourri of different personalities as well. Because of that, it made coaching them an exciting experience. Looking back, I remember sizing them up as follows:

Kyle Brentley was the most athletic player on the team and by far the best player. He was average height with a stocky build that more resembled a fullback than a point guard. Kyle was going to be the go-to guy; when the game was in jeopardy, the ball was put in his hands. Kyle was also a very tough, fearless kid who most of the time sported a flat-top (marine-style) haircut. As I have already mentioned, he was of average height, so quite often when he would drive to the basket, he was smaller than most of his challengers. This never stopped Kyle, though. He was as gutsy and determined as they come.

If you were to imagine Speedy Gonzales hyped up on Mountain Dew and six candy bars, it would describe the motor that Chad Nelson had going continuously. There was not a player alive who Chad could not catch no matter how much of a head start he had. I have seen him literally run a player down who had already made it past half-court before Chad even started after him. He was absolutely the fastest player on not only our team but in the entire league. That, however, was where his basketball skills began and ended. Chad was not only the fastest player in the league, he was also the shortest. He looked so little on the floor that one could not help but think he was playing in the wrong league. Chad could not shoot the ball very well either. His shot looked more like a "chuck" than an actual shot. His dribbling wasn't much better either, but on defense, he was unstoppable. I would put him in just to create havoc for whoever was bringing the ball down the floor.

Ryan Nichols was as large and tall as Chad was short and tiny. He was a beast of a child. Ryan stood a good head above our next tallest player. He was just simply a big kid. I believe his shoes would have been too big for me. He eventually became known as "Yeti" to myself and the other players. I remember seeing him for the first time and wondering why in the world the other coaches would pass on this boy. And then I saw him shoot. He missed the rim. He was slow, could not shoot the ball, could not dribble, and was by far the weakest player on the team. I believe I once saw Chad (half Ryan's size) push him out of the way so he could grab a rebound. I felt sick to my stomach.

Brian Peterson was also very small. He was skinny, weak looking, and did not display very good basketball skills. Brian Peterson was, however, very intelligent, gifted, and advanced. Great. Could I not just get a shooter? However, even with his small size and lack of athleticism, he soon became fun to coach because he was very funny.

I REMEMBER ONE GAME, I was stressing over the way we were playing, and I decided to call a time-out to emphasize a point. When the team returned to the floor, Brian turned back to me and winked. "Don't worry, Coach, we got this," he said. It was obvious that Brian was going to need a lot of work, but it also became very obvious that I was going to love working with him.

Wil Payne, like Chad, was very small. Wil was both skinny and short. He did not have much strength and often appeared to totally freak out when the ball was tossed in his direction. He would actually duck away from the ball as if he was afraid of it. This kid was going to need a lot of work. The positive thing about Wil was that he was always smiling and having fun—except when the ball was passed to him.

Pete Self was an average-size kid. He displayed some ability to both dribble and shoot. He had a tough disposition about him and did not take any crap from either players or coaches. Stealing the ball from Pete would ultimately result in you receiving an out-of-control, angry player in your face. Pete, like the rest of the team, was going to need a lot of work. The one positive thing that I noticed about Pete was that he could follow instructions better than any of the other players. If I had to design a special play during a time-out to help us score, Pete would be the one who I would want to handle the play. He just seemed to grasp what I would be trying to develop quicker than anyone else, although he never let on like he did or that he even cared.

Of course, being the Great Eight would actually require us to have eight players, and I am sure you noticed that I was only able to recruit seven. Our eighth player actually showed up the night of our first practice. He was a move-in—his family moved to our location from a different county during the school year. Therefore, he escaped the notice of the other coaches. He was an unknown. There are moments in our lives where, when looking back, one can honestly say that things happen for a particular reason. You can call it destiny, godsent, or divine intervention, but I can tell you that when Reed Messer entered the gym and ended up on our team, that was one of those moments. We went last in the selection order, resulting in us having the fewest players, which allowed me the next player if one showed up, so Reed Messer joined the Wildcats. Coincidence or fate, either way, it was one very fortunate thing to happen to the blue team.

Reed was an above-average-sized kid. He was very athletic and had one tremendous motor on him. He was Kyle, Ryan, and Chad wrapped up in one. I am not saying that he was as good a ball handler and shooter as Kyle. He wasn't as big as Ryan, nor was he as fast as Chad, but he was a little of all three players in one body plus the toughness of Pete. He was a beast and soon would be one kid the entire league would get to know and have to reckon with.

So with Reed rounding out the blue team, we now had the Great Eight. Now you have been introduced to my team, but as far as understanding their greatness, the following chapters will help you appreciate why I consider them great and how we overcame many challenges in order to come together as one special team. *The blue team. The Wildcat team. The greatest team to ever step onto the hardwood in the basketball-rich state of Kentucky.*

CHAPTER 6

Practice Begins, as Do My Headaches

SINCE WE HAD THREE TEAMS now competing for practice time, our gym-time assignments were broken up into three different practices about one hour and fifteen minutes each. We had Tuesday evening at seven and any other time that was available, which was almost never. The school was not a sports-oriented school by any means, and the principal would not go out of her way whatsoever to arrange extra time for our boys to practice. That meant if we wanted to practice more than the allotted hour and fifteen minutes, it was up to the coaches to accommodate that. And it was at our own expense as well. This amazed me. What principal would not want to advance his or her school's athletic programs by supporting the coaches' efforts in teaching the children by at least providing a place for them to practice? Well, that's all I need to say about that at this time.

The first Tuesday practice was quickly upon us, and as I drove to the school, I began to arrange in my mind just how practice would go that night. Visions of players keenly in tune with my instruction, executing flawlessly every basketball drill I threw at them kept floating around in my head. Players going hard to the basket, making one-handed shots from three-point range, and dribbling the ball with great skill was how I envisioned the evening would play out. I had worked out various strategies: how they would overcome any man-to-man full-court or half-court press and how to destroy a 2–3 zone defense by making the extra pass. I could see it all in my mind. The players would sit on the floor, quietly hanging on every word that left my mouth, and then, like a well-oiled machine, they would execute every drill precisely as instructed and masterfully. Then I arrived at the gym.

The first hint of reality was the loud, piercing sound of children screaming at the tops of their lungs. My brain just could not comprehend what my eyes were beholding. There were kids everywhere fighting on the floor, climbing the bleachers, and throwing balls at each other. And in that entire mess were my kids, some crying in the middle of the floor—all except Pete Self, who had a poor victim in a headlock banging the child's head into the hardwood. Wil and Ryan were spinning in circles muttering some strange child language, and Rocky was vomiting in the bleachers. I spun around looking for those responsible for these monsters, and that's when it hit me: the parents. I had yet to meet any of the parents, and they were there just staring at me as if I have already lost control of practice, which, in all appearances and practicality, I had. I froze like a Popsicle. Terror had just overtaken me.

Keep in mind that the whole Penn State/Jerry Sandusky scandal had just broke on the news, and now here I was, an utter stranger, taking control of their second-grade boys without their parents knowing anything about me. Imagine having that rolling through your mind while you are standing there in a catatonic state on the gym floor staring back at the parents of the kids that are creating helter-skelter behind you. I felt as if

I was going to be sick. I managed to visually span the bleachers looking for some set of eyes that would offer assurance as to say, "Hang in there, Coach. We are with you." There was none. Just blank stares—some angry and most others confused. I tried to introduce myself to them, but instead of words, just mumbled grunts and groans passed through my lips, reminding one of Carl from the movie *Sling Blade.*

As I was standing there in utter shock, speechless, staring up at the parents, Dustin approached me and asked, "Are you ready to get started, Coach?" I snapped out of the sick trance I was in and looked at him bewildered.

"Are you ready to get started?" he repeated.

"Hell, yes. Let's get them on one end of the floor for some drill explanation."

I was completely grateful that Dustin was assisting me. He knew most of the parents and would be instrumental in our ability to get their trust and support once I could get the introduction out of the way. That night surely did not impress anyone, but that is pretty much how the first practice went. Once we settled the kids down—and you will never know how blowing the whistle can do just that—we began our dribbling drills. This allowed the kids structure and instruction and afforded me the opportunity to continue evaluating the players.

As practice continued, I noticed an older kid sitting in the bleachers by himself watching us. He would look away when he saw me look up at him. After some time watching us practice, he got comfortable enough to help me out in his own way. At times he would toss a ball out to me or bring me my clipboard. He would help some of the players during drills. I approached him and found out two things right away. One, he was extremely shy and very nervous when I engaged him in conversation. Two, he loved the game of basketball more than anything but was never athletic enough to make a team. His father was the janitor for the school and allowed his son to help out where he could in the gym. After clearing it with his father, I asked the kid if he would be interested in being part of our team helping out as equipment manager and as an assistant. After much convincing and comforting from his father, he agreed to help. His name was Frank, and he became a valuable asset to our team.

The "Wildcat"

OUR PRACTICES CONSISTED OF BASIC layup drills, dribbling drills, box-shooting drills, defense, rebounding, and foul shots. As was discussed earlier, the previous year's team seemed to just run the one player that could dribble the ball, and the rest of the players would get out of his way. I wasn't going to do that. I wanted to first create and then implement an offense that would involve all five players. It would be a motion offense of sorts. With eight-year-olds, cleverly giving the play a cool name was as important as the play itself. So I named it the "wildcat."

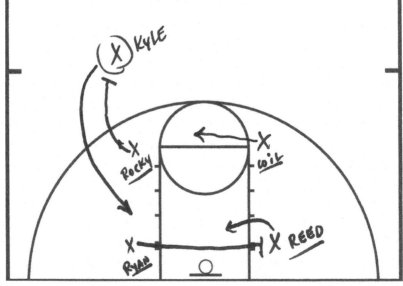

If you understand basketball, then this will make sense to you; others may want to skip ahead. The No. 1 point guard calls "wildcat." Then No. 2 sets a screen for No. 1 as No. 5 crosses the lane and picks for No. 4, at which point No. 4 runs off the pick and goes across the lane toward No. 1, who is dribbling down the lane after being picked by No. 2. As a result, the point guard has the option of driving to the basket or passing the ball to No. 4, who will be open in the lane as the point guard approaches. This can be run to either side toward the No. 2 or No. 3.

This play creates movement from every position, requiring all of the players to get involved in the offense. We also taught our kids every position so we could put them into the game at No. 1, No. 2, No. 3, No. 4, or No. 5. This way they could not only relieve any player on the floor but also understand the role every position has. This turned out to be very successful for our team.

We also taught another play, which was a pass to No. 5 at the foul line and No. 1/No. 2 would split the post, but the wildcat became the play that we would run the most. We even used it to pass the ball inbounds from under the basket. I remember the father of one of our players approaching me during practice and expressing his concern that the wildcat was just too complicated for the boys to understand. I simply looked at him and said if we didn't teach them basics like picking, screening, and cutting to the basket, when would they ever learn it? All they knew from the previous season was to just get out of the way of the guy with the ball. I then continued with our practice.

I also focused on attack defense. We were more than likely the smallest team in the league, so I knew we had to be the most aggressive if we were to succeed. These boys learned to attack the dribbler and challenge shots and to box out their opponent, allowing them to get the most rebounds. We ran the fast break on the opponent's missed shots and ran our offense when the other team scored.

I felt that we had a strong plan in place, and with some time, we could tweak these boys into a decent team. I was wrong. During our second practice, Dustin approached me and said, "I just found out that we start playing next week," as he showed me our schedule.

"What are you talking about? These boys are nowhere near ready."

"Well, ready or not, Coach, they have a game next Saturday," he said.

I couldn't believe it. These boys still needed so much more work. It would take a miracle to get them ready to play after just two practices. So at the beginning of practice I gathered the boys together in the middle of the floor and explained to them that we would be playing our first game the following week.

"Boys, in order for our team to be ready to play, we really have to practice hard and pay extra attention to what the coaches are saying. If we don't practice hard, well, then we will probably get killed. We don't have any additional practice time before we play, and I am concerned that you guys just are not ready yet. So prove me wrong tonight," I said.

Then I stared at their faces, expecting determination and nods of agreement as if they were saying, "We are with you, Coach. You can count on us." Instead, I got blank stares, with Chad staring at the ceiling and Rocky picking his nose. This was going to be ugly, I thought.

CHAPTER 7

Game No. 1

I HARDLY SLEPT THE NIGHT before our first game. I kept running various strategies through my mind that might assist us in defeating our first opponent. This was not going to be an easy game. We were taking on a seasoned team that had played together since kindergarten and was very familiar with how this league operated. I, on the other hand, was a rookie and an unknown who didn't have a clue as to how this league operated. I really did not know what to expect. Did I need to keep a book, create a lineup sheet, or work the scorer's table? How many time-outs was I allowed? How were the players going to substitute into the game? These questions and others caused me to toss and turn all night.

The morning of the game I got out of the bed early and went to the kitchen to fix some coffee. I sat down at our kitchen table and wrote down the starting lineup for the day along with the substitute schedule. This process would become my Saturday morning routine. It allowed me time to play the game in my head to determine which player would be best at particular times during a playing period. Since we played six-minute quarters, I decided to substitute at the three-minute point of each quarter unless I needed to pull someone from the game earlier than that due to fouls, laziness, or inability to follow instructions.

Once completed, I went to my room and dressed for the game, gathered my game book, and headed out the door for the gym, which was about a fifteen-minute drive from my home. I decided to get to the gym about an hour before we were scheduled to play. As I slowly got closer to the gym, my stomach was turning into knots. I am sure this is what every coach who has reached his first game in a new town experiences. Finally I arrived. They gym was very old and looked considerably dated from the outside. I would guess the building was built in the sixties by looking at the red brick, and the parking lot was quite small and mostly unpaved. The building itself was very plain looking. The classrooms adjacent to the gym had exterior walls of windows, which were all cluttered with the latest art projects the class was assigned. My hopes were that the inside was much more appealing. It wasn't.

The school was Crestview Elementary, and it just so happened to be who we were playing that morning, with the added pressure of playing them on their own gym floor. This was how our season and my introduction into this league were to begin. Now my stomach was really starting to turn. As I entered the building, I noticed that in the foyer and through the hallways you pass a glass case filled with trophies. All were basketball trophies, strategically placed by the entrance, giving any traveling opposing coach a certain degree of intimidation. At least for me it did. My stomach kept getting worse.

I passed the concession area, climbed the stairs, and went through another set of doors that, due to the sound of shoes scuffling the hardwood, the scoreboard buzzer, and the official's whistle, convinced me that this was the gym. I entered.

Like the outside of the building, the gym was also very old. Wooden bleachers climbed up about ten rows toward the ceiling on both sides of the floor. Below was the hardwood basketball floor with old benches on the sideline for coaches and players. One end of the floor was an open stage for school plays and pep rallies while the other end was a brick wall that in my opinion was too close to the basketball goal—not a lot of room for a player running the floor for a layup on that end. A player would have to jump at an angle to prevent colliding into the wall.

The basketball floor divided the bleachers in half. One side of the gym was for the home team and the other for the visiting team. I didn't know which side I needed to be on. It's funny how one's mind can play tricks on him or her while under stress. As I entered the gym for the first time, carrying my ball bag and game book in my hands, I felt as if every eyeball in the entire gym were on me—as if the game actually stopped and everyone, including the officials, coaches, and the players, turned to see who this strange man was walking into their gym. This, of course, was not actually happening but was simply my nerves getting the best of me.

At the end of the bleachers, I found a place to sit and wait for our game to begin. As I sat there, I watched the game scheduled before ours. Their players looked really good. The coaches were barking out instructions as the players flew up and down the court. I became very impressed with their skills and their ability to score. These two teams would be difficult for us to beat.

After several minutes of watching the game, I noticed Dustin, Rocky, and his mother, Rachel (who after a few games became our other assistant coach from the stands), enter the gym. I waved them over to me. At this point, I realized that I could use someone to discuss our game with, and Dustin was my target. Besides, I needed to bounce the substitute schedule off of him.

"You ready for the game?" he asked.

"No, I feel sick to my stomach. I don't remember being this nervous for my own games back when I played."

"You'll do fine; just try to keep them under control, and you will have a shot. By the way, I have to leave. I just got called in to work, so good luck today. I thought I would come by and wish you luck," he said.

"You got to be kidding me. I can't handle these kids by myself. What the hell are you trying to do to me?" I yelled. "Dustin, you have to be here to help me at least run the bench. My stomach is already tore up; I don't need any additional stress. Call in sick or death in the family, I don't care what you tell them, but you have to be here to help."

"Sorry, Coach, I have to leave right now, but I wanted to wish you luck," he said as he got up, leaving me with Rocky and his mother sitting there and staring at me.

This is freaking perfect, I thought. *He's leaving me on the day of our first game and me not having a clue what to expect.*

I didn't know what to do in regard to getting someone to help me, which I desperately needed, but it really didn't matter at that point because just about then, the game buzzer went off. *Oh no*, I thought, *I didn't even think about gathering my players together prior to this game ending.* I looked around for my players, and then, just like bees leaving the hive, they came running out on the floor from various places in the bleachers where they were sitting with their parents. That was my first and would soon be my last relief for the day.

I looked at Rocky and said, "Form two lines, and let's do some layups to get warmed up."

Rocky ran onto the floor to the other players and gave them my instructions. They perfectly formed two lines and started doing layup drills.

My attention quickly turned to the opposing players, who were at the other end of the floor running through their practice drills. It didn't take long to see that they were much bigger, quicker, and more talented than we were. *Great,* I thought, *not only are we unprepared, but also much smaller than they are.* I felt sick.

We continued with pregame drills until the buzzer sounded again letting the coaches and players know that the game was ready to start. Wil's father offered to help me on the bench, and I was so grateful for that. I gathered my players into a huddle on the floor by our bench. I felt like Coach Norman Dale from the movie *Hoosiers*, starring Gene Hackman as the head coach. I was much older than the other coach, and older than any of the coaches in our league, for that matter. I was nervous and wasn't really sure what to say to my team. I grabbed the lineup and read it to the players, letting them know who would be starting the game.

"Rocky, Kyle, Ryan, Reed, and Wil are my starters, and the rest of you pay attention to who they are guarding because in three minutes, you will be going into the game," I instructed. "Let's go, boys; play hard and remember our offense. Let's run the wildcat at them and attack on defense. Ryan will jump for tip-off. Okay. Go, blue, on three."

"One, two, three."

"Go, blue," they yelled.

As the players broke huddle and headed to the center of the floor, my sour stomach started to return. The official positioned the players around the circle and was ready to toss the ball into the air. It was more obvious, now that the players were standing next to each other, that Crestview Elementary was a much bigger team. They looked like giants next to my boys. But my boys were warriors, fierce and tough. They were seasoned players who would not be pushed around. A quick sense of pride started to fill my heart but was short-lived.

The official tossed the ball into the air, and the game, the season, and my Saturday mornings for the next eight weeks began. It was as if time had stopped, and the ball just held there in suspension, dangling in midair. It looked like

something right out of the movie *Matrix*. Then I was slammed
back to earth when the much taller Crestview player smashed
the ball out of midair toward one of his players, who was prepared to take it down the floor. My players freaked out. Ryan
was still looking for the ball that was crushed past him by his
opponent. Kyle was down at the wrong end of the floor. Rocky
was running in circles as Reed just stood there staring at him.
Frank was vomiting into the opponent's bleachers, and Pete
Self was standing toe to toe with one of Crestview's misfortunate players ready to strike. I felt the room spinning, heard
laughter behind me in the stands, and thought I was going to
follow Frank's cue. I just stood there frozen again, watching
as pure terror swept over me. The Crestview player who received the ball ran the length of the floor and scored the first
basket of the game (a mere fifteen seconds into the season) as
my players simply lost it. Just fifteen seconds into the season,
we were totally losing it. *Do something*, I kept telling myself.
Do something!

I jumped up, yelled, and signaled for a time-out. The official, after giving me a look of disbelief, blew his whistle and
sent the players over to their coaches. I knew calling a time-out
just seconds into the game wasn't the smartest thing a coach
could do, but I also knew that I had to settle these kids down. I
knelt down inside the huddle and looked at my players. Blank.
My mind went completely blank. I just stared up at them blink-
ing. I was blowing it. I was supposed to be their inspiration,
their rock, and the one they could count on when things were
not going well. Instead, I stared at them wondering where I
could hide or how I could sneak out of the gym. Then it hit me.
Run the wildcat. Just run the wildcat. And, for whatever reason, that was the one and only idea that actually brought some
comfort to me. Amazingly, I was able to speak in an articulated
language other than a mumble.

"Fellas, settle down. You have to just settle down and concentrate on what we practiced," I screamed.

"We have to run the wildcat," I continued. "When we inbound the ball, stop staring at the ceiling and running in circles, and please stop picking your nose. Get down the floor after we inbound the ball and set up in the wildcat offense. Go, blue, on three. Ready. One, two, three."

"*Go, blue!*" they yelled as they broke the huddle and went back out on the floor.

And then, just like it was scripted, Kyle called out, "Wildcat." He broke to Rocky's side as Rocky set the pick for Kyle. Kyle broke free. It was a clear, unguarded lane all the way down to the basket. We all saw it. It was beautiful. I could hear parents yell from the bleachers, "Go, Kyle!" He dribbled full speed toward the basket and went up for the uncontested layup. There wasn't anyone for miles there to stop him. The wildcat worked perfectly. Kyle's little arm extended out, delivering the ball to the basket, and it bounced off the front of the rim. We all stood there in amazement at what should have been an easy two points, but instead the ball sailed off the front of the rim through several hands and to the floor, where the next amazing thing happened.

Somehow Wil was able to gather himself back from the spells of a nervous breakdown and reached down for the ball. After securing the loose ball, Wil then turned toward the basket and heaved the ball toward the goal. The ball hit the rim, rolled around the inside of the rim, and eventually fell through. The gym exploded into a roar of excitement, yelling, applauding, and laughing. The smallest kid on our team and in the gym had just scored the first basket of the season. This was the kid who just moments before had been spinning in circles staring up at the ceiling. It was a miracle. We were tied with Crestview, and now we were in the game.

I looked down the bench at Wil's father and yelled, "Where did that come from?"

"I have no idea," he said as he stared out on the floor, grinning with pride at his son, who for that brief moment was the hero of the game.

Son of a— I thought as I pondered briefly the moment that we just witnessed.

Wil ran back down the floor smiling as well. As I mentioned in the beginning of this book, greatness comes in many forms, and in that particular snapshot in time, greatness was experienced.

We were tied at two after the first quarter. By the end of the second quarter, our team settled down, and scoring became more frequent as a result of both our wildcat offense and our pressure attack defense. By the end of the game, Crestview could not hold on to the ball whatsoever against our defense. Time after time, Kyle would strip the ball from one of their players and would drive the lane to score a basket. Reed was also creating havoc for their players with his steals and rebounds, and he was scoring often for us. The game soon ended, and we finished with a close 11–10 win against the much-larger and more experienced Crestview. As we lined up to shake their hands, I noticed that the Goliath Crestview players looked as if they had just come from a war. *Pete must have gotten to several of them,* was my first thought. They were utterly beaten. This gave me the idea to proceed with our smaller team as a team that would wear opponents down with defense. We were going to be more aggressive and quicker than our opponents. My plan for the rest of the season had just presented itself to me, and I for once was starting to understand.

As we left the gym, parents and coaches congratulated me for our success. I was starting to feel like a coach. Even TJ and Bryan approached me as I was exiting the gym and congratulated me. Of course, as my mind works, they were just there to scout me and the team to see what offense we would run. It is amazing how things just work out. Walking into the gym that morning, I would have bet we were going to get destroyed by Crestview. Then, exiting the building, I felt as if we were invincible. Just four quarters (or twenty-four minutes), a eight-feet-six rim height, a 27.5-inch ball size, and the Great Eight changed my thinking. Isn't it funny how little things like that can change your entire outlook?

CHAPTER 8

Game No. 2—Old vs. New

THE WEEK FOLLOWING OUR FIRST game was busy. I had arranged for an additional hour of practice from the school, which was nearly impossible. Gym availability in this county is scarce and is allotted out by importance: first the high school boys and girls get the gym time needed, followed by middle school athletes, cheerleaders, volleyball players, and then us.

I intended on working the boys hard on the wildcat and another play we threw together that they had struggled with during the previous week's game. During practice, Dustin approached me and said, "You know who we have Saturday, right?"

"Yeah, the white team. Why?"

"And you know who coaches them, don't you?"

I stared at him for several seconds, lost in the simple fact that I had completely forgotten that we were facing the man who had coached these same boys last year—the one man responsible for Dustin's request for me to coach this team. The one man who I'm sure had one goal in mind—destroy Coach Sully's Wildcat blue team. This game took on a whole new importance. I had to beat this man in order to validate my existence as this team's coach, or at least in my own mind anyway.

"Get the boys ready for defensive drills, Dustin. I want to shut this white team down." Dustin smiled as he walked away blasting off his whistle along with several commands for the team.

We drilled the boys very hard that week, reminding them who they were facing in the next game, and how nice it would be to beat this team. We also stressed to the team that they were going to have to play their very best in order to win on Saturday. The white team was a very good team with a couple of standout players. Strict execution of fundamentals and of our offense would be required in order to pull off this upset. Then I got the call.

"Hey, Coach, this is Reed's mother. I am calling you to let you know that Reed will not make the game Saturday. He is going to be out of town for the holidays but will be back in town for the next game. Have a good Christmas."

"You got to be kidding me. What kind of mother are you that would do this to our team? We need Reed this week, and if you take him out of town, we don't stand a chance against the white team. If he does not play Saturday, then don't bring him back. He's off the team," I said on the inside, as I panicked.

"Okay, Mrs. Messer, thanks for letting me know," is how I actually responded.

I was faced with playing this game with one of our better players not being there. I decided to run Pete in Reed's position during the week's remaining practices and informed the rest of the team that they had to be at the game Saturday. I was running short on players.

The Saturday game day came quickly, and, to my surprise and relief, not only were all of the players there (minus Reed Messer), but Dustin was there as well. I was starting to really enjoy arriving to the gym Saturday mornings hearing the sound of distant feet scuffling against the hardwood floor and the familiar sound of the official's whistle and the game clock horn going off. The aromas of various foods from the concession stand filled the air. No doubt the menu would consist of culinary masterpieces such as cotton candy, hot dogs, and cheese nachos. I enjoyed seeing the parents of the various teams wearing their school colors and displaying their school loyalty with face tattoos of their teams' mascots. And, of course, the sight of one of my team assistants again vomiting on the other team's bench. Yes, nothing smacked more of Saturday Youth League basketball than these little things.

I met Dustin on the floor, and we proceeded with instructing our team into their pregame drills. I was quite impressed with the team's ability that morning to knock down the majority of their shots. They were missing nothing. I remember thinking that we could actually have a tremendous game if we could come close to duplicating these put-downs. It was impressive to watch, but I soon noticed that it wasn't just me watching. Bryan and his assistant were in the middle of the floor watching everything my team was doing. No doubt they had heard about our outstanding performance last week and had to see just who they needed to be concerned about. The way my boys were hitting everything they put into the air, they should have been worried about this entire team.

I approached Dustin.

"Did you notice who is studying us?" I said.

"Yes, they have been scouting us ever since we took the floor. I guess they are trying to figure out who is guarding who."

"Or trying to get a look at the plays we are going to be running." My paranoid mind only allowed me those types of thoughts.

"I don't think so," Dustin said. "If that was the case, he would have been scouting you last week."

"I think he did, actually," I said. "It doesn't really matter anyway. We are getting ready to start the game," I added as I watched the final pregame seconds tick off the clock. The horn went off, and we were ready to play. I quickly got the kids into a huddle.

"Boys, listen. We are playing your old coach today, and, well, it would just mean a lot to me if we can beat them, so you will need to play your very best."

Dustin went over the starting lineup, and then we put our hands together. "Go, blue, on three. Ready. One, two, three."

"Go, blue!"

With that, they headed to center court for jump ball.

The official tossed the ball into the air, and we got first possession. "Wildcat, wildcat!" I yelled. Kyle drove to the right, which was Rocky's side of the court. He called "wildcat," and Rocky set yet another perfect pick. Kyle drove straight to the basket uncontested for an easy layup and dribbled off his foot out of bounds. The white team quickly inbounded the ball, and down the floor they charged for a score. We quickly raced back up the floor with a nice pass to Ryan Nichols, who promptly turned toward the basket and took a shot. It didn't even hit the rim. This was consistently repeated time and time again throughout the entire first quarter. It was as if we had used up all of our made baskets in the pregame drills. Now, we couldn't even throw the ball into the ocean if we were standing on the beach. Kyle, after one of his attempts driving to the basket, drew a foul from one of the white team's players. He lined up for two foul shots. His first shot sailed through the air and missed the rim. His second shot was good, and we finally had our first points of the game.

Shortly after that, the quarter ended with our team down 6–1. I told our players that we just needed to slow down and concentrate on getting the ball into the basket. I informed them that our offense looked good minus the fact that we could not make a shot. I thought our defense was very good. We just needed to slow down on our offense and concentrate harder. We settled down for the second quarter, and we ended the quarter being down 5–3. The third quarter our defense was beast-like, denying the offense any attempt at making a basket. Ryan was swatting shots out of bounds like a hillbilly swatting flies that escaped a bug zapper. Both Kyle and Pete were denying passes and making steals time and again. The quarter ended with our team taking its first lead, 4–0. We shut their team out for the entire next quarter, and with just one quarter remaining to play, we would need another defensive effort like the third quarter in order to win the game. Our team was down 11–8 going into the final period.

The fourth quarter looked a lot like the third quarter with one exception. We went ice cold again in terms of not making any baskets. Our defense was awesome again, but we just could not produce enough points. And even though we were able to limit them to just two points, we could only manage a few points for the entire quarter.. Because of the lack of points in the fourth quarter, we were never able to overcome the margin of defeat in the first quarter and ended up losing the game by one point, 12–11.

I made the humiliating march of defeat over to Bryan, feeling like General Lee surrendering to General Grant, and congratulated him for his victory. He shook my hand and thanked me, but I thought I detected a smirk on his face as he passed by me. My first thought was to turn Pete loose on him, but then I simply realized that this win must have been as important for him as it would have been for me. Actually, the pressure had to be on him to win and validate still being the coach. That made me switch gears in thinking, and I began to dwell on the boys' effort that day. The more I thought about it, the more encouraged I was that my team could rally back after being blown out in the first quarter to making a good close game of it. Bryan must have been sweating bullets. Dustin and I exited the building and made our way to a local restaurant, which soon became a regular Saturday lunch hangout, and ordered food washed back with some suds. We discussed the game over and over again. We finally agreed that the outcome would have been much different had Reed been playing and that would be evident the next time we played them. We also noticed that the next week's game would have the same pressure and would offer even more of a challenge. We were playing TJ's team. My stomach started turning once again.

CHAPTER 9

Game 3 vs. Another Previous Coach

WE SPENT THE WEEK WORKING on our offense, shooting drills, and playing tight defense without fouling. It was becoming evident that a couple of players on my team were starting to display difficulty in not fouling the opponent. As a matter of fact, this problem had reached the director of the league's office, and he was reconsidering the "no keeping track of fouls rule for kids this age." So we were told, but, nevertheless, I was making a point at each practice to work on good defensive technique.

As weeks went by, I noticed a couple of my players were starting to have difficulty making it to practice on time or at all. I had one rule when it came to practice—you practice, you play. No practice, no play. If a player was sick or was delayed to practice due to something out of his parents' control, I would allow that, but my goal was to put an end to the showing up when or if they wanted to, including, and mostly, the parents. As a result, I had one player in particular who could have been a starter, but he missed too many practices and also several games. He missed practice that week, which meant that I would probably be one short again on Saturday at our game against the gold team.

Saturday's game was a chance for me to redeem myself from

the previous week's devastating loss to their former coach. I had to make sure that we were very sharp with both our offense and our defense. I was able to secure some extra practice time, and I felt that our boys had worked very hard during the week. I thought that we should be ready.

Kyle was developing into quite a point guard and definitely was the best point guard in the league, in my opinion. He was fearless and would somehow squeeze himself with the ball into the tightest spots only to break free for a basket. He was and still is to this day a fun kid to watch play this game. Ryan was developing slower by this point than I thought he would be. He was a giant among these boys but still had trouble keeping the ball above his head, and he continuously had problems with the dribble. What I loved about him was he always had a smile on his face and had the best attitude. He was impossible to yell at—it just didn't work with him. Reed was developing quite well also. He was fast and had a scorer's instinct. Besides his fouling, his defense was second to none. Rocky was playing much better also. He had several shot attempts that missed, but considering he never was given much playing time the previous year proved that he had come a long way. Rocky was very task oriented. When I told him to pick, he picked quite well and put the opponent to the floor. Chad was still going a million miles a minute and creating a living hell for whoever he was guarding. Chad could stick on a player better than anyone. Wil and Brian were coming along as well but not as fast as the rest. They were very smart kids, and once they entered the game, they knew exactly what to do. They still needed work on both dribbling and shooting. The reason I am offering a progress report on the status of my players now is that I was going to need 100 percent out of each and every one of them in order to win the game that Saturday against the gold team.

Game day began as most Saturday mornings did. I would

normally rise early and start some coffee, which eventually would fill the house with its aroma, along with the pound of bacon and eggs I typically prepared. I enjoyed going over my lineup while slopping down the good stuff. When I was finished cooking, any hopes of anyone sleeping in were over.. That thick aroma filled the entire house. Poor Tobie—she was a basketball widow in more ways than one.

I was exploring different lineup arrangements, hoping to discover a group of five that I hadn't previously considered, but I kept coming back to the original five. We continued to struggle with scoring in the first quarter of each game. Unfortunately, I knew that in order to defeat TJ's team that morning, we would need a big first quarter.

I wrapped up the lineup and the substitution sequencing and then headed toward that old red-bricked gym that was about to host our game. As I approached the entrance, I was once again lured in by the whiff of cotton candy and hot dogs. I was really starting to like this place. I entered the gym and found Dustin sitting with Rocky in the bleachers.

"Hey, guys, how are we doing this wonderful morning?" I asked.

"Good, Coach. Do you think we can beat them today?" asked Rocky.

"Only if you play your very best and so do the other players; then, yes, I think we can beat them," I said as I gave Dustin the "I hope so" look, and with that the horn went off, signaling our turn to take the floor.

We huddled up, and I gave out my instructions as to how we were going to play this team. The boys seemed very excited and ready. They lined up for jump ball, and with the sound of the whistle, the game began, and so did my concerns about winning.

The gold team outjumped us and then ran the length of the floor for an easy layup. Within twenty seconds they took the lead. We answered with Kyle tripping over his own feet, falling to the court, and giving the gold team the ball. Again, they ran the length of the floor for another easy layup. I signaled a time-out.

"What's the matter with you guys? You're letting them just run down the floor for layups. Where is our defense?" I shouted. "We practiced hard preparing for what I told you they would do, and now I want to see it on the court. Settle down and get into our offense. Most importantly, don't let them score any more baskets. Blue on three. One, two, three."

"Go, blue!" they yelled.

The rest of the quarter was tight, but with a 4–0 lead on us, we were running out of time to chip away at their lead. Then Chad got a steal and threw the ball down the court to a wide-open Ryan, who scored, making it 4–2. Now we were cooking. After several trips up and down the floor without either team scoring, Reed fouled gold's best scorer and put him on the foul line. The first shot went through, but the second was short. We had one last attempt at scoring, but the ball didn't find the rim, ending the first quarter at 5–2 and our team in another hole.

After the first quarter, we huddled together, where I continued to emphasize the need for our team to settle down and concentrate on our offense. I switched a couple of players' defensive assignments due to Dustin's recommendation, and that turned out being the right call. The second quarter seemed very similar to the first. We allowed some easy baskets and struggled on our end to score any points. I was beginning to think we were jinxed when starting a game. The second quarter ended with us scoring two points and the opponent scoring four points, which put us down 9–4 for the first half to the gold team. We were going to have to turn this around in the second half or face losing to yet another coach from the previous year's team.

The Huddle

I huddled the team up and instructed them on how to run the wildcat and the man-to-man defense, and on the simple fact that we were not playing very hard. They were outhustling us, playing harder defense, and getting all the loose balls that hit the floor. I reminded them that they were playing a very talented team, and the way you beat a talented team is to outplay them. The boys seemed to understand as they took to the floor for the start of the second half.

I thought I detected an entirely different attitude in these boys. They weren't afraid anymore. They weren't nervous either. I just remembered that I didn't even see Frank puking upon entering the gym. No, these boys were not intimidated at all by the gold team starting the second half. They were just mad! That caused me to quickly turn, and I immediately looked to make sure Pete was on our bench. He was, thank God. But he also looked angry, as did all of our players on the bench.

The whistle blew, and we were handed the ball. Kyle took off like a bullet all the way to the basket for an easy layup. So much for us getting off to a slow start. Reed stole the ball and raced down the floor for another layup. Up 4–0 in the quarter,

I took a peek down the sideline at TJ, who was staring back at me. Then Kyle came up with another steal and ran down the floor for another basket and a 6–0 lead for the quarter; TJ called a time-out. Within seconds you could hear TJ blistering his team's ears for the sloppy and unaggressive play. I knew what he was going through, just experiencing the same thing with my team during the first half. Of course I used the time to find out what had changed my team's attitude.

"What has gotten into you guys?"

"We're tired of getting beat," Ryan said.

"Well, good job, boys. This is what we have been waiting to see all season. We got them on the ropes now, and they're scared, so let's keep the pressure up on defense—no easy baskets. Challenge every shot. Blue on three. One, two, three."

"Go, blue!" echoed off the gym's walls. With that I sent both Pete and Chad into the game.

It was the last thing the gold team wanted to see. Chad is just a maniac around the ball. He will eventually get the ball from you, and he did this time. Pete is, well, Pete is just scary. He was wrestling boys to the floor for loose balls, which seemed to please him greatly. Before you knew it, the third quarter ended with our team leading 10–4 for the quarter, which put us up for the game 14–13 with just one quarter left to play. I pulled the boys together and told them this was it. If they wanted to beat this team, they would have to continue playing hard, just like they did in the third quarter.

The fourth quarter began, and it was very close. We started out with a basket, and then they would answer with one of their own. This continued for the entire quarter, and we never let up on our defensive pressure; nor did we waver on our wildcat offense. And at the end of the game, as both coaches glanced up at the scoreboard, our blue team won, 20–17, as we were able to eke out a triumphant fourth quarter, 6–4. I kept staring at the scoreboard, lost in the moment, and causing Dustin to pull me away to line up and shake the gold team's hands, which was customary after each game. As I approached TJ, I extended my hand to him and said, "Nice game, Coach."

He looked at me and smiled as he said, "Nice game, Coach; welcome to the league."

With that exchange, my attitude toward both TJ and Brad changed entirely. These coaches didn't have an agenda against me at all. They truly wanted me to succeed. Obviously they were just cautiously allowing me to prove myself with these young boys. This entire time it was just my crazy competitive and paranoid mind that had me thinking otherwise to start with. So as I exited the building, putting behind me the smell of leather, sweat, and cotton candy, and the sounds of hyped-up second-graders, I had a sense of purpose and the feeling that I belonged here coaching this team. Funny how a sweet victory can cause just that. Go, big blue, indeed!

CHAPTER 10

Another Chance at a Normal Life

As WE INCREASED OUR DAYS of practice during the week, my energy level kept depleting. I would come home from practice and collapse on the couch. Ironically, it was my team's stamina that I had been concerned about one week prior, and now here I was wondering if I had it in me to finish the season. Basketball had actually become a distraction from my heart condition and overall lack of energy. Then one day, a friend suggested meeting with the cardiologist with whom she worked. He was known for taking on difficult cases and would take a look at my catheter imaging to offer a second opinion about procedures that might be available to me. This initially did not appeal to me due to an unsuccessful online second-opinion process with the Cleveland Clinic, which resulted in a wasted year of forwarding information to them. So after some consideration and a lot of convincing from Tobie, I agreed to meet with him.

The new cardiologist was an all-business type of doctor and did not offer much in the way of small talk, so it was very difficult getting comfortable with him. He spent a considerable amount of time reviewing my case and studying the film of my last catheter imaging, which was now about eight months old. After quite some time, he began discussing his recommendation. He felt that he would be able to reopen the occlusion and set a medically treated stint into the artery, keeping it from closing up again, but the procedure had the typical risks. The risks included punching through my artery, sending me screeching straight into surgery for an emergency bypass. His justification was simple and true. He said I was too young to be put on any medicine that restricted me from activities. I had to take the risk. We scheduled the procedure for the following week.

Before we knew it, it was the day of my procedure. The cardiologists were going to run a wire into a vein in my groin area (i.e., catheter). Then they would insert the stint into the closed artery. If everything went well, it would take about forty-five minutes. I lay there on the operating table watching some cardiologist fella struggle with getting the catheter wire to punch through the clogged artery. I remember thinking that this procedure was not going to work. After several minutes struggling with the catheter, my cardiologist came into the room, and within fifteen seconds he was through the clog and was able to stint me. I was instantly impressed and relieved. I returned to the recovery room for an evening of observation. The next morning, I was released. I was amazed at how much better I felt, and after a couple of weeks, the beta-blockers were thrown into the trash. I was back, and I had a team to coach. I had the Great Eight counting on me. So, to the dismay of Tobie and the shock of a couple of parents, I scheduled practice for the next day—just two days after my procedure. I felt great, and we had a game to prepare for! I was back.

"The will to succeed is important, but what's more important is the will to prepare."

—Bobby Knight

CHAPTER 11

Starting to Come Together

THE WEEK OF PRACTICE IN preparation for our second game against Crestview, we needed to work on several things. Dustin and I knew that Crestview's coach, having already played us, would have his team more prepared this week. The wildcat would only trick a defense the first time we played a team. The second time around, coaches could easily defend against it.

I was able to secure another gym to give us an extra night of practice, which we used to work on pressure defense, giving special attention to not fouling the offensive player. This we were becoming prone to do and had become known for fouling a lot. A few of my players were sick, and I was informed Friday night before Saturday's game that Pete would not be playing on Saturday due to illness. I also got a call from Chad's parents informing me the same thing. This was going to create a very short bench, leaving me with six players total.

So we practiced the six players hard in preparation for Saturday's game. Crestview had one player in particular who took the majority of their shots. He was a very good player, and he gave us fits guarding him the first time we faced him. Crestview liked to screen high on the point guard, similar to our wildcat, and then drive to the basket. Unlike our wildcat, their guard never looked for the pass but instead, once he made his break around the screen, he was going to take the shot.

We showed our boys the "switch" technique against the screen. When the player you are guarding runs to the top of the key to set a pick for the point guard, you yell "switch" and then literally switch the player you are guarding for the point guard coming off the screen. It may not stop him from scoring, but it certainly slows him down considerably.

Saturday morning was game day as usual. I fixed breakfast once again, polluting the entire house with the thick smoke and aroma of burnt bacon and eggs with extra-strong coffee. I also looked at my lineup for any possible changes, but none was found. With just six players that day, the boys were going to have to play a lot more than they were accustomed to, and I knew they were going to be tired. I would have to rely on some time-outs to get them both rest and water. Dustin had his work cut out for him.

I finally made my way to the gym, and while driving there, I realized that Rocky had yet to score. As a matter of fact, he hadn't taken many shot attempts lately. Then I remembered promising his mother that I would make him a much better player, and here we were a few games into the season, and he hadn't scored even a goal. I could barely keep my assistant coach Frank from physically losing it let alone teach a nonaggressive kid to get more involved in scoring a basket. Today would be a great opportunity for him to start. I would have him get the ball and try to score or get a rebound and put the ball back up. Either way, his days of being content with someone else taking the shots were over starting today.

I made it to the gym and found Dustin and Rocky sitting in the bleachers along with several of our players. I approached Rocky and said, "I want you to take a shot at the basket today."

"I don't know," he said.

"Rocky, if you are ever going to improve your game, son,

you have to get involved in the offense. Just get in there when we take a shot and get a rebound. Then all you have to do is turn toward the basket and let it fly. You have great form, so you should be able to score. Most of our points come from rebounding the ball after we take a shot and putting it back in."

I could tell he was nervous as he kept saying, "I don't know, Coach."

"Okay, promise me this, then. You will at least get an offensive rebound today. Let's start there, and then the shots will come later, okay?"

"I will try, Coach."

Dustin added, "You have to remember, most of these kids just sat on the bench last season and were not allowed to touch the ball, let alone shoot it. They were told if they got their hands on the ball that they were to give it right to one of the coach's main players. So they don't really know how to get into the offensive rhythm."

"That changes today," I said. "I want all of these kids to have an opportunity to score before this season is over. I want all of our players to make it into the books this year even if we have to change our offense to accommodate that."

The horn signaled the start of our game. My team took the floor and got ready for jump ball. It still amazed me even being four games into the season just how much smaller we were compared to these other teams. With the exception of Ryan, who was just a beast, my players were smaller at every position. The official threw the ball up in the air, and the game officially began.

We won the tip-off, and Kyle set the team up for the wildcat. He called the play and drove to the basket, only to miss the layup. It was a great opportunity for Rocky to get the rebound, but he was already starting down the floor.

Crestview's coach had figured a way to slow our wildcat down, which both Dustin and I knew would happen. So after yet another slow start to the first quarter, we were down 8–4 to Crestview. I pulled the boys together before the start of the second quarter and went over the switch defense. I wanted our pressure defense to start only after we switched who we were guarding. I thought we could lull them into thinking they would have a lane off the screen right to the basket, but instead we would be able to switch, forcing the point guard to turn, allowing us to steal the ball—or something like that. These were just second-graders, for God's sake. No tomahawk dunks coming from any of these boys, but that would make for one heck of a story.

We took the floor again to start the second quarter. This time our boys were able to run the switch defense and caught Crestview completely off guard. Their point guard would come around his screen time after time only to run right into a wall of blue players standing there waiting for him. It frustrated him so much that he left the game sobbing uncontrollably. Now I am not the type of person or coach who enjoys seeing a kid losing it like that, but I will say there was a degree of satisfaction knowing our boys were defending like they were taught, and also causing such havoc on the opposing point guard that it forced him to leave the game. I must have been grinning ear to ear because as I watched that guard leave the game, my eyes met the eyes of their coach, who was standing along the sideline, and he was not happy. His face was red with anger, and I do believe if he could have gotten his hands on me, he would have done some serious harm. The quarter ended with our team ahead 5–4 during the quarter. It was halftime, and we were down in the game at this point 12–9. Even though our defense was much better in the second quarter, we still were struggling with both getting our offense going and then hitting open shots. Rocky still had not shot the ball.

Before we took the floor for the second half, I called the boys to the huddle and gave them my instructions.

"Boys, we need to keep the pressure on them. Keep the switch pressure defense going—do not let up. I don't care if their entire team leaves the floor crying. We will not back down!

"Also, Kyle, I want you to run the wildcat to the other side of the court. I know we typically run it to Rocky's side, but I want to change it this half. Run it to Wil's side of the floor. That just might throw them off enough for us to get a clear lane to the basket. Understand?" I asked.

"Yes, Coach," they all agreed.

"Okay, blue on three. One, two, three."

"Go, big blue!" they yelled.

We were handed the ball, and Kyle started toward Rocky and then switched toward Wil as he yelled, "*Wildcat!*" This put Crestview in a disoriented state. As Dustin and I figured, they had only practiced guarding the wildcat when ran to the one side, thus leaving the other side practically unguarded. Kyle shot to the basket off of Wil's pick, and there, all alone, stood Ryan right under the basket. Kyle sent a bullet pass down to Ryan, who turned and scored.

Crestview's coach was calling out some help to stop Ryan but could not get it done in time. As they were trying to figure out what had just happened, Reed got a steal and put the ball back into the basket for a quick 4–0 lead in the quarter. Crestview called a time-out. We never let up from that point on. We pressured them so hard that their point guard did not make it through the third quarter before heading to the bench, once again in tears and mumbling something inaudible. This game was going to have a lasting effect on this kid similar to the post-traumatic stress syndrome that our troops face when returning home from war. The quarter ended with our team winning the quarter 7–0 and putting us ahead for the game 16–12.

I could tell our team was anxious to start the fourth quarter, like sharks in the water tasting the blood of some misfortunate sea creature. Crestview, on the other hand, looked more like that injured sea creature. They were shaken and whipped. Their point guard and leading scorer did not come back on the floor.

The fourth quarter continued on like the third quarter did with the exception of our missed shots. With only six players and our style of play, we were tiring out quickly, like an automobile running out of gas. I was becoming concerned about our team's stamina and ability to finish this game. However, despite the fact the boys were physically spent, our shots started falling. Our feet, however, were getting slower, which allowed Crestview to score. By the end of the fourth quarter, we had just enough to win the quarter, 6–4, and the game, 22–16. We lined up on the sideline and approached Crestview's team, offering our hands for a congratulatory high five. Everyone on their team slapped my hand with the exception of their coach. He would not even make eye contact with me. I congratulated him just the same on a hard-fought game.

I left the gym that morning a victor for the second straight week. I learned a lot about our team that day. I learned that they had the guts to stick out a tough game. They had the desire to win regardless of the pain they may be experiencing. They were starting to become a group of coachable kids resurrected from the land of basketball chaos, which we witnessed at our first practice. They were really starting to listen to the coaches. Their parents were starting to really support us, even spending more time talking to Dustin and me. They began joking with us and getting involved in the practices. These boys were becoming a good team right before our very eyes, metamorphosing from the sloppy, out-of-control brats they once were. They were becoming a fun team to coach and slowly were becoming the Great Eight.

CHAPTER 12

Game 5—Hold On to Your Seats

WE WERE REALLY LOOKING FORWARD to this Saturday's game although we were going into this game blind, since we did not have a chance to see this team play. From what the other coaches told us, they were pretty good, with one really good ball player who could kill you in the paint. That meant I had to get Ryan playing better. As I already mentioned, Ryan was a beast in size. He was a man among boys. The problem with Ryan was he was weak and did not possess an aggressive bone in his large adult-sized body. He was not able to get tough rebounds or muscle the ball into the basket. He simply was too nice. Dustin and I worked with him to get him somewhat stronger, but he was still having issues with bringing the ball down below his waist, allowing a smaller defender an opportunity to take the ball from him. Ryan was going to be a work in progress and would require the full season to correct his bad basketball habits. But I loved coaching this kid. He always had an exceptional positive attitude.

After making a few minor adjustments to our offense, I felt pretty confident that we were ready for Saturday's game. It also looked like I would have my entire team healthy and able to play the game as well.

Saturday came, and after polluting the house with toxic breakfast smoke, I headed for the gym. I was greeted by Dustin as I entered the gymnasium.

"Have you noticed how big this team is?"

"No, not yet," I said. "I haven't had a chance to scout them."

I then looked at the Canyon Elementary boys and was amazed at the size of these players. They looked like junior high school players. We were definitely outmatched height-wise, and they looked a lot bigger and stronger than us as well. They were all about Ryan's size. We were going to need a huge game from him that day.

"Well, perhaps that just means they're a lot slower than us," I said with a look of embarrassment as the words left my lips. I could feel Dustin's eyes burning holes into me, so I chose to just make my way to the floor and get the team warmed up.

The official signaled for our team to take the floor. Imagine a two-story house nestled in among the skyscrapers of down-town Manhattan. That is how my boys looked trying to match up with Canyon Elementary players on the floor. The size ad-vantage they had on us was tremendous, and I can remember hearing some of their parents sitting behind me laughing and joking about how small our team was. I was about to protest when the official tossed the ball into the air, and the game began. With Ryan being so nonaggressive, I had Reed do jump ball. He was able to outjump the Canyon player, and Kyle re-trieved the ball and started down the floor. He called out "wild-cat" and ran it perfectly. Kyle shot to the basket and scored. Canyon Elementary came down the floor but was quickly picked off by Reed, who ran to our basket and scored. The points started coming easier, and before I knew it, the quarter was over with our team leading 8–2. This was unbelievable, especially since we customarily struggled with scoring in the first quarter. I wasn't sure what to say to the boys during the time-out other than "Nice job, and continue playing hard."

The second quarter started out the same as the first with our offense clicking on all cylinders. The combination of Reed's defensive efforts, which resulted in easy baskets, and Kyle commanding the offense like "Stormin' Norman" did his troops during Desert Storm left Canyon Elementary baffled. Nothing worked for them. Every time we came down the floor, we either scored with ease or missed wide-open shots, and there were very few of those. I decided at the beginning of the season to substitute players halfway through each quarter, or at the three-minute mark. I wanted the bench players to know when they were coming into the game so they could pay close attention to who they would be substituting for.

Finally we reached the three-minute mark, and I signaled for our substitutes to enter the game. Pete, Chad, and Brian ran out onto the floor. I decided to give Kyle a rest along with Rocky and Reed. It was a risk taking my two main scorers out of the game, but I needed to rest them. This, by the way, did not go unnoticed by Canyon's coach. He immediately inserted his best player back onto the floor after initially signaling for him to sit. It would be up to my bench players from this point on in the second quarter.

They too were relentless. Before long, Chad had their point guard in tears after causing him to turn the ball over continuously. Pete, being the ferocious intimidator, was getting in on the action as if he was putting his foot on the throat of a struggling prey. He came up with the ball after forcefully taking it away from the Canyon player and started down the floor. Pete didn't bother calling a play. He didn't need one. Instead he drove straight to the basket with a look in his eye daring anyone to try to stop him, and nobody did. Canyon's defense just got out of Pete's way. It looked like the Red Sea parting as the players simply stepped aside as Pete dribbled to the basket and scored.

The quarter ended, and so did the first half, with our blue

team leading 22–2 over the much taller Canyon Elementary. At this point, Dustin and I decided to rest our starters more than we typically had to allow our bench players additional minutes to play, giving them more game experience. I pulled the team to the bench and explained all of this to them.

"Guys, you have done a great job. That first half was better than all of our games put together. Way to play hard, and way to be focused. Now I'm going to play the bench more this half to give them more experience at various positions."

"Did we do something wrong?" Kyle asked.

"No, not at all. I just want—"

"Why do they get to play more?" Reed asked.

"I want to give them extra time when I can so they can get more comfortable."

"We played really hard, and now you're going to bench us?" Kyle stated.

"That ain't fair," Reed complained.

"I don't want to sit on the bench," Ryan added.

"Why? You think we can't handle them?" Pete said as he started toward Ryan.

After grabbing Pete, I explained, "*Listen!* We are destroying that team, and it's not good sportsmanship to keep running the score up on them. We have already won this game. Now is the time to allow some of our bench players time to play. That is what I believe in, and that is how I coach, and that is how we are going to do it. Period. Now all of you will get to play this second half, but the bench players will be getting the majority of the playing time. Is that understood?"

They muttered and nodded yes. The second half was getting ready to start, so I sent my starters in to get things started. I instructed Dustin to substitute intermittently after two minutes.

The second half was difficult for us. We started missing shots, and they started making them. We fell behind for the first time in the game. Kyle had a few turnovers to start the quarter and was ice cold from the floor. After two minutes, we substituted Pete for Kyle. Pete played the way he did in the previous quarter. The kid had no fear, but then again, it was Pete, after all. And then it happened—the ball was passed to a wide-open Rocky. He turned and heaved the ball up toward the basket. As if in slow motion, the ball slowly crept through the air. Dustin and I were side by side holding on to each other. I was yelling, "Go in. Go in," as Dustin was screaming, "Get in there." The ball hit the back of the rim, rolled around the rim, and then back out to the backboard. It then rolled back around the rim and eventually fell out to the right side. It was as if all the air got sucked out of that gym as everyone gasped. It looked like that was going to be Rocky's first basket of his career.

My head dropped as I stared at the floor. I was in a deflated trance, and then all of a sudden the entire gymnasium broke out in a loud cheer and applause. I looked up and saw our team running back down the floor. We made a basket. But who? Rocky's shot did not go in. I turned to a smiling Dustin, and he knew that I had no clue who scored the basket, so he said, "You won't believe this, but Pete went flying into the paint from the three-point line, took the ball out of their player's hands, and put it back into the basket for his fourth point of the day."

He was right. I could not believe it. I was sad that Rocky missed his shot, but I was greatly appreciative of Pete's hard play. The quarter ended with Canyon ahead 12–8 for the quarter and our team winning the game 30–14 at that point.

I decided to leave the subs in the game to start the fourth quarter and then bring the starters into the game if needed. I was soon rewarded for that with outstanding play from our subs. Pete was able to pick up another basket, and he finished the game with six points. Kyle had his biggest game of the season with eighteen total points. When it was finally over, we won the quarter, 10–4, and won the game, 40–18. It was the most points scored by a team in our league so far that season. It was also one of the biggest margins of victory by any team that year. We were now a team that the other coaches took notice of. Soon we would notice other teams running their version of the wildcat. Word was getting out that the blue Wildcat team was very aggressive, very quick, liked to foul, and had several boys who could score. Now they could add one outstanding bench to that as well.

After huddling with the team for an aftergame discussion, I dismissed them and said good-bye to their parents. I caught up to Dustin and Rocky on my way out the door.

"You guys want to get some lunch?" I said. "I'm in the mood to celebrate."

"Sure," Rocky said.

"Where do you want to eat?" added Dustin.

"Let's try that Mexican restaurant you like out in the county. I would like to discuss today's game and next week's game with you. I am so excited about how these boys played today, and, Rocky, way to take that shot."

"Sorry I missed the basket, Coach," he said.

"Don't you worry about missing shots now, Rocky. You just keep shooting the ball. Eventually, they will start falling through the nets."

We headed out for lunch with Rocky under my arms in a headlock, and once again I had the glow of victory on my face. To date, our team had just one loss, and, more importantly, we were starting to play really well. I could not wait to get back on that floor. This was coaching, and I was starting to really enjoy this. So I thought.

CHAPTER 13

The Tidal Wave Meets the Boys

PRACTICE WAS GOING TO BE difficult. I had decided to turn up the pressure on the team because we were about to face the toughest team in the league. We were facing Pond Creek Elementary, and they were legendary. They had three exceptional ball players and five other really good players. There was not a weak spot on their entire team. It was also the home of the best elementary basketball player in the entire tri-state area. This kid could literally shoot from anywhere on the floor. He was very tall for his age and strong. He could consistently hit three-point shots, layups, foul shots, and jumpers. He had a knack for finding the open player on the floor and bullet passing him the ball for an easy basket. He was also a ferocious defender. If you shot the ball anywhere near this kid, the shot was getting blocked. The way he attacked the ball made Chad look like a kindergartner, and the way he rebounded missed shots would intimidate even Pete. Somehow, we were going to have to get past all this and organize a game plan. So we worked hard on switch-and-help defense, trying to focus on the best player and closing him down. I thought our defense would be sufficient, but we would need to score a lot of points to stay with Pond Creek. We worked on the wildcat over and over.

I was confident that we could play with this team, and I thought if we can play with anyone, then we can beat anyone as well. I was overconfident, it turned out.

SATURDAY GAME DAY ROLLED AROUND, and I was off to the gym. I felt somewhat similar to how I felt when I first arrived to the gym for our first game. I was a nervous wreck. I entered the gym and right away spotted Frank throwing up in a trash can. I guess he was having some similar nerve issues, as well as several hot dogs, it appeared. I was just happy he wasn't doing this on Pond Creek's bench. As I entered the gym, I noticed Dustin had the team already doing warm-up drills. Since we were the first game, we were able to start warm-ups as early as we wanted.

Just as I was starting to think I had a handle on my nerves, Pond Creek took the floor. And so did my jaw. They were huge. Think David versus Goliath in size disadvantage. We looked like the little Hickory team in the movie *Hoosiers* when they went up against the large 5A school in the state championship game. Not only were they large, but they were burying every shot they took. They were impressive to watch. They were one well-oiled machine—just like clockwork, running through their drills meticulously. It wasn't just their skills that were impressive; it was their uniforms. They were a spotless purple with gold trim. In history, the color purple denotes royalty, wealth, and power. Standing there watching these boys go through their warm-ups, I could not think of a more fitting color for this team to wear. I looked back at my own boys and noticed half of them had their shirts inside out, while the other half didn't have them tucked in at all. Some had their jerseys half-in and half-out. And we were missing about seven out of ten of our shots. I could only imagine what the Pond Creek coach was thinking.

They were athletic, well-dressed, well-coached, and came with an entourage of fans and cheerleaders. They blasted music for their workouts prior to the game while I, on the other hand, considered it a treat to just keep Frank from getting sick or Pete from scrapping with someone on the floor. They were ready to put on a show at our expense, and I needed to figure out a way to slow them down and needed to think of something fast. The whistle blew; I was too late with coming up with an idea.

We huddled up, and I reminded them of who we were playing and that I wanted to slow the game down. I told them we did not want to run the floor with these guys. I instructed them to set sharp picks, block out on rebounds, and pressure their point guard. We took the floor. The official threw the ball up, and Pond Creek controlled the tip. Now at this point I was standing at the sideline watching the players. By the time I turned and took a seat on the bench, we were down 4–0. I quickly got back on my feet to assess just what the breakdown was, and we went down another basket, 6–0. I called a time-out.

"What's going on out there?" I yelled.

"You guys are not getting back on defense, and they are running you out of the gym!" Dustin pointed out loudly.

"Okay, boys, just settle down and run your offense. Once you score a basket, the game will settle down some for you, but you need to get that first basket."

"Wildcats on three. Ready—one, two, three."

"*Wildcats!*"

Kyle tried over and over to get the offense going, but Pond Creek's defense was just too solid. When he could break through, the shots would be so difficult that he could not put them down. Reed and Ryan were no help either. They played like Kyle in that when they could get free from the defense, the shots just did not fall. The quarter ended, and we were down 10–0.

I was embarrassed, angry, and frustrated, and I let it out on the boys. In my opinion they were playing in an intimidated and lazy way. I laid into all the boys about the need to play harder and play smarter. We simply were not protecting the ball, and we were not hustling down the floor. After a much-needed tuneup, I sent the boys back out to face the much bigger Pond Creek. I noticed my boys sweating profusely, out of breath, and bending over, resting their hands on their knees. Pond Creek, on the other hand, looked as if they had just come back from a nap.

The second quarter found both teams actually battling it out. We found the ability to score the basket and to defend better. I think our team just needed to settle down some and let the game come to them. In the previous quarter our boys were shell-shocked, and that caused them to rush their shots a little. By the end of the second quarter we found some rhythm but unfortunately lost the quarter 5–4. We were down for the game, though, 15-4.

We discussed the first half and worked through some additional drills. The boys were somewhat down due to the thumping we experienced at the hands of Pond Creek. I reminded them that the only way we could overcome this was to play harder and to pressure them into making turnovers. Really though, we needed to improve in all aspects of the game in order to make a serious run at winning this game. I kept a positive display of hope during our discussion, since I did not want the boys to detect any inclination of hopelessness from their coach.

The second half started out neck to neck. We were having trouble not turning the ball over, but our defense had improved enough to the point of causing Pond Creek to turn the ball over as well. The third period ended with our team losing by four points, so even though we were narrowing the gap, it was essentially impossible to win this game. We were already getting beaten badly at this point, including being blown out in the first quarter, so I had an idea.

"Okay, boys, here is the plan. We are playing pretty competitively with them at this point, so let's set a goal to just win one quarter today. There is one quarter left, so let's try to win this for our school. What do you guys think? We have one last quarter where we leave nothing on the floor. If we play our guts out these next six minutes, then we can win, proving to everyone that we belong here and can beat this team."

I thought that I had given the best motivational speech of my short coaching career, and I expected that these boys would go through the roof with excitement. There would be no containing them now. I began to mentally pat myself on the back and pour the "attaboys" on myself when I suddenly became aware of something. There was no response. I could literally hear the crickets chirping outside. They must have not heard me.

"Well, what do you guys think? Can we win this quarter and show everyone who we are?" I asked.

"We're tired, Coach, not sure we can do any more," Kyle said.

"But you haven't done much of anything all day. Anything would be an improvement," I said.

"They're too good. We can't beat them," Wil chimed in.

"Okay, boys. Let's just forfeit the game and not even try to win the last quarter," I said loudly as I started packing up our gear.

"Coach, we will try to get them for you. We'll do better." Ryan must have detected my frustration and anger because he huddled the rest of them together before heading out to the floor.

I proceeded toward the bench, sat down, and then lowered my head toward the floor in disbelief; suddenly I felt a little, skinny arm resting around my neck. It was Brian Peterson smiling at me.

"Don't worry, Coach," he said. "We got this." He then headed back out to the floor and turned back, looking toward me, and winked. Amazing. Here was one of my kids with the least amount of talent, not to mention his lack of size, but he definitely had the biggest heart. I really enjoyed coaching this kid.

I looked down the bench at Dustin and asked, "Can you believe this?"

"It's just not our day, Coach. We are missing too many shots, and in order to defeat this team, you need to hit most of your shots. We will pull it together next week."

"I don't want to wait until next week, Dustin. I want to win this quarter."

Nothing else was said as we began the fourth quarter. Both teams competed pretty evenly. We would make a little run, then Pond Creek would make a run. The game stayed tied with ten seconds to go, and Reed Messer got fouled while attempting a shot. He was going to the foul line for two shots. That was it. Reed never misses, and with just seconds left, my boys would be able to provide me with a victory in the fourth quarter. The first shot went up and in. We had the lead for the first time this entire game. We went up 5–4 for the quarter. The second shot banged off the side of the rim right into a Pond Creek player's hands. He took off like a rocket toward his end of the floor. With six seconds left, he crossed the half-court line. He was the kid that Reed was assigned to guard, and Reed was nowhere to be found since missing the free throw. As my other boys began picking up the players they were guarding, it left this Pond Creek kid with the ball wide open with three seconds left crossing the foul shot line. Two seconds left, and he lets it fly toward the rim. The buzzer goes off just as the ball falls through the net. And just like that, Pond Creek won the fourth and last quarter, 6–5. I was furious.

Our team lined up to congratulate Pond Creek, and we then proceeded with the high fives for their players and coaches.

Afterward, when I would typically give some departing advice or criticism, I just packed our gear up for the second time and headed toward the door. I stormed past several of our players and parents without saying a word. I simply could not get out of that gym fast enough. Dustin looked at me and, realizing I was in an angry state, did not engage me in postgame conversation. I did, however, notice the dejected look on Rocky's face, but I simply did not have the capacity to comfort him. I had earlier agreed to meet Tobie at the local mall for some shopping, which I was now regretting. I felt as if my head would explode.

We met inside the mall at the food court, and I informed her that I was in no mood for shopping and was going to sit right there and eat something. She could tell that I was very aggravated and rightly decided that shopping alone would be a better option for her. I found a food kiosk, selected a large pretzel and soda, and then found an empty table at which to sit. This was definitely the highlight of my day. As I ate, I kept thinking about the last play of the game. How could we just give them that basket when really we had the win in our hands and just ten seconds left? Why did Reed blank out after missing the last shot? Why did nobody bother stopping that kid driving toward the basket? Was it my fault? Was I a bad coach? Would I be able to get this team back together and playing good basketball? Did I even want to coach anymore?

So as I sat there drowning in my mental torture of self-pity and doubt, I noticed out of the corner of my eye two little boys approaching my table. They were wearing blue sweatpants and blue hoodies. As they reached my table, they pull their hoodies back. There stood Wil and Brian.

"Hey, Coach, what are you doing here?" they said. I noticed their parents securing a table for their families.

"Well, I was just in a mood for a pretzel," I said. "What are you guys doing here?"

"Mom needed to shop for a few things," Brian said.

"That's great, and I'm really glad to see you two."

We talked for a little while longer before they had to go and eat with their families. There we were sitting in a shopping mall food court, Brian on one knee and Wil on the other, just hanging out and talking. We didn't talk about the game, practice, or anything else to do with basketball. We just talked, and it was exactly what I needed to bring my feet back to earth. At that moment I realized that this team wasn't about me, as if it were some insignia that I would wear on my chest to show off my coaching skills. It really wasn't about winning, either. Sure, everyone likes to compete and win, but that wasn't what we were all about. Coaching our team was about taking eight kids and teaching them a sport. It was about teaching them how to play together. It was about teaching them how to get along with one another. It was about respecting one another and other players in the league as well. It was about taking eight misfits—undersized, underskilled, and outcoached players—and making a good team out of them. It was about improving week after week. More importantly, it was about having fun, and that was where I was starting to lose it. It was starting to be clear to me. To be successful with these boys, I could not just be a coach to them. I had to be their teacher, leader, and friend as well.

For many fans, the game of basketball is bigger than life itself. It is huge in the world of sports. The game's most remembered players are usually the Goliaths of the sport. Seven-footers like Kareem Abdul Jabbar, Shaquille O'Neal, and Yao Ming have given fans many memories and lessons throughout the years. So it seemed quite ironic that the basketball lesson that I was receiving was coming from my team's smallest players. They were four feet nothing and maybe fifty pounds each. Brian and Wil were teaching me that this game is just a game, and these players were just young boys, after all. I needed to keep it fun for them. I remember sitting in the food court that day promising myself that from that moment on, these boys would get better. They were going to learn more about this game, but more importantly, they were going to have fun doing so. And I was going to start having as much fun as possible also. I was starting to transition from the blue team's coach to the blue team's biggest fan.

CHAPTER 14

Round Two of Old vs. New

Dustin and I huddled up in a corner of the gym after practice and discussed the week's game because we both knew that TJ would not allow us to beat him twice in one season.

"How do you want to play this one out?" asked Dustin.

"We can run wildcat like we have done all season, but this time I'm going to have Kyle run it to the opposite side. Perhaps they won't be ready to defend it from both sides of the floor."

"You may want to come up with something new to throw at the gold team. If I know TJ, he will have that team ready to defend the wildcat anywhere on the floor."

"I know, Dustin, but it makes me nervous to introduce another play to them this late in the season, and our number-one play is not working at all. I will have to figure something out."

I knew that Dustin was right, of course, but I was reluctant to change our plays in fear of creating mass confusion with the boys. After several evenings of changing, then rechanging, then only to change it again, I decided to just leave the wildcat the way it was but drill the team to run it sharper than ever. The week's practices would be focusing on running the offense over and over until we could run it with each player knowing how to run every position. The team practiced very hard; they were determined. To them, the games against the other teams in their school were the most important. Apparently a feud over basketball bragging rights permeates throughout the schools, even into the second-grade boys' ranks.

Our record to date was four wins and two losses. This game could very easily make or break our season. We still had two very difficult games left in the season, and if we lost them, we would finish .500 with four wins and four losses. We could also finish with six wins and two losses, which would be one incredibly successful season given the fact that these boys hadn't even had one win the previous year.

Before I knew it, it was game day. I rose earlier than usual that morning to begin my pregame ritual, which was starting to become a joke with the neighbors. It was as if the Catholics were watching for the white smoke to exit the chimney at Conclave, signaling that a new pope had just been appointed. Black bacon smoke would exit the door with me, with the usual symphony of several smoke alarms accompanying the odor. I would just smile and salute all onlookers as I made my way to my truck clasping in one hand the raw and nearly dead carcass that was supposed to be breakfast. God, I loved Saturday morning basketball.

I ARRIVED AT THE GYM earlier than usual, hoping to catch up on a game being played before ours. As I entered the gym, Dustin and Rocky pulled into the parking lot. I waited for them to catch up with me.

"Did you get much sleep last night?" Dustin asked.

"Yep, just like a baby. I cried all night and wet myself," I joked.

"You wet yourself, Uncle Sully?" Rocky asked.

"No, genius, I was just joking with your dad."

"Did you make any changes to the plays?" Dustin asked.

"No, Dustin. I just want to run with what we got. I fooled with different options all night, but in the end, nothing really worked for me. So I am leaving it alone."

Second Time against Gold Team

As I EXPLAINED EARLIER IN the book, our school has three different basketball teams for our age group (blue, white, and gold). All three teams play against each other in the same league. So playing each other makes it extra stressful because these kids have to go through a week of ribbing if they lose to their schoolmates. This helps to motivate them during the week of practice, but it adds extra anxiety for the coaches because we know how important these intraschool games are to these kids.

It wasn't really who we were playing that was concerning me that morning as I approached the old building that would house the arena of battle between two lethal second-grade combatants. It wasn't the pressure of defeating a coach who had coached one of the teams the previous season. It wasn't even the sight of Frank hunched over the garbage can enjoying his game-day routine. Frank now just waves at me from his bent-over position every time I enter the gym and call out his name. He usually gets the attention of the janitor, who stands by Frank with a mop extended out to him as if to say, "I am not cleaning this up." What was really concerning me was the boys' inability to score many points. We designed a play that put them into position to score, but our team still missed too many easy baskets. I knew that in order for our team to beat the gold team again, we were going to need every basket we attempted, or it would be a very long morning.

Dustin was making his way to the bleachers when I entered the gym. I approached him and took a seat next to him.

"So are you ready for the game?" he asked.

"I think so, but I am concerned about our struggle to score

points. The boys have been missing an awful lot of easy baskets of late. You know TJ does not want to lose to us again, so he will have his team ready to defend against the wildcat."

"Oh, yeah, he will have that team ready. Do you want to throw in a surprise play for him or just go with what we got?"

"I am not worried so much about our team getting a shot off as I am about our ability to score baskets. I don't think anything new will do us any good if we can't score. They are just going to have to play through this slump and defend hard," I said as we watched the game being played prior to ours coming to an end.

It was time to take the floor and go through our warm-ups.

As our boys ran through their pregame layup drills, I again noticed that we were not scoring many of our layup attempts. Still concerned, I turned to watch the gold team go through their drills. Perhaps they were struggling as well, which would have convinced me that I was worrying too much about nothing. I was wrong. This looked like an entirely different team from the last time we met on the court. They were determined and focused, as player after player began to put the ball through the net. TJ was running the drills like a conductor over a symphony. It was beautiful and flawless. He masterfully barked out commands, instructing his players to the basket. Player after player was burying the ball in the basket on every attempt. They appeared serious and focused in every step of each drill. Their eyes were replaced with orbs of fire looking red hot as they gazed upon our players with disdain. There was no horseplay, conversation, or joking around. They were here for one reason—to destroy the blue team!

No big deal, I thought, as I turned back around to behold my own warriors. Surely they were as focused and intense with eyes of fire ready to devour the gold team. Kyle just missed a layup. The ball sailed over the rim onto the stage behind the goal. Ryan just shot an air ball. Pete was holding Chad down on the floor, banging his head into the floor. Dustin was screaming at Rocky for missing an easy shot, and Frank—well, you know what Frank was doing. Again visions of Buttermaker from the *Bad News Bears* started surfacing in my head. I called the team over into a huddle, where I proceeded to verbally chew their little faces off.

"What's the matter with you guys! This team will kill you, and half of you are over here goofing off. We barely beat this team the last time we played them, and since we have not been shooting the ball very well lately, I thought you would take this more seriously! But I guess you don't care, so this morning, I am starting my bench players."

The regular starters, who would not be starting the game, shouted out their disagreements along with some other choice words and took their seats on the bench. I worked with the three who would be starting that day—Chad, Pete, and Bryan—until the horn sounded, signaling time for the game to begin.

The official's whistle went off, and the game began. Within seconds we were down 2–0. The gold team was sharp that day, and our team once again couldn't throw something into the ocean if they were standing on the beach. Halfway through the quarter I got my starters into the game. The quarter ended with our team playing much better defense, but we still were down 6–2. We were still struggling to make baskets.

The second quarter went back and forth defensively, both teams not wanting to give up anything. We had our chances running the wildcat, but this team was better prepared for us this time. The second quarter ended with our team scoreless and down 2–0 for the quarter. We only scored two points for the entire first half, and we were now down 8–2 for the game.

We made some adjustments at halftime, and I told the boys that the only way to overcome a slump is to shoot your way out of it. We just needed more shots in the second half, and we would be fine. Of course, this was total BS, but I had to come up with something that would get their minds off of missing baskets.

The third quarter started out like the second quarter had, with neither team producing much offense at all. Our defense clamped down on the gold team, and their point guard in particular. He was our major scoring threat, but following the first quarter, he could do very little. Kyle was on him like Frank over a trash can. The quarter ended tied at 2–2. That meant we were down for the game 10–4. That was a lot to overcome with just one quarter left. I pulled the boys into a huddle and told them we needed to keep pressuring their guards. We also needed to focus on our shots and to slow our shot selections down some. I thought that we might be rushing our shots too much.

The fourth quarter was our best quarter of the day. The team had a determined look in their eyes and developed a swagger, especially Kyle. I noticed that he did not let anyone drive past him when on defense. The boys really turned the pressure up on the gold team's guards, not allowing them any baskets at all. Our offense improved tremendously as we started running the wildcat to the opposite side, resulting in several uncontested layups. Kyle had the ball driving down the floor with one minute to go. He drove around his screen and was wide open all the way to the basket. Kyle drove in and laid the ball up off the backboard. It twirled around and fell out. Ryan was there to scoop it up, and he took a shot that bounce off the back of the rim. Reed ran the ball down and turned to shoot as the game-ending buzzer went off. The ball never made it to the rim. We won the quarter 6–0. I wasn't sure about the game until Rocky's mother came over to the bench and congratulated me on the tie.

"What? Are you sure?" I asked.

"Yes, I am sure. The final score was 10–10."

"So do we play another three minutes or something to see who wins?"

"No, you just end in a tie. No extra periods allowed," she said.

After congratulating TJ and his players, I headed for the exit. I was going to meet Tobie, Dustin, Rocky, and Rachel for lunch to discuss the game. *Wow, this is what a tie feels like,* I thought. *No real satisfaction or disappointment. Just emptiness. I probably would prefer to be blown out. At least then there would be some kind of emotion and determination upon the ending of a game. A tie, on the other hand, just sucks.*

I entered the restaurant and sat down at the table with Dustin and his family. He looked up at me and said, "Well, we pulled that off today."

"What do you mean 'we pulled it off'? We didn't pull anything off other than a stinking tie. Wow! If we could have hit just one more basket, we would have swept TJ's team. We didn't accomplish anything with a tie. It's as if we didn't even play the game."

"Well, you could look at it that way if you want."

"Is there any other way to look at it?" I snorted.

"You could look at it like this, if your pride will allow you to. TJ is a very good and respected coach in this area. In two different attempts he was not able to beat your team one time. Even when he knew exactly how we were going to play and which offense we would run, he could not best you. A tie against a team like that and against a coach like that to me means you found a way not to lose the game, Coach. You are new around these parts, so when parents see how you scrap and fight for every game, it means a lot to them, and it means a great deal to us also. You refuse to lose, and that's starting to rub off on our players. They played their guts out today."

There I sat with my head down, Tobie angrily glaring at me. Just a week prior, in that mall, I had vowed to start making this game fun for these boys, and here I was, just seven days later, pouting over a stupid tie. He was absolutely right, of course. TJ was a very good coach and had been involved with this league for several years. The fact that he had not beaten me never crossed my mind.

Dustin was also right about my pride. The boys played much better in the second half, and there I was, fuming over how the game ended in a way other than what I wanted. I could build off this game and take it into our final week of practice in preparation for our last game of the year.

"You are so right. I am very sorry, and I never considered that. Thank you for getting my head on straight, and, yes, that is a much more exciting way to look at today's game."

"No quitting now; we have one more game left, and you know who it's against, don't you?" he asked.

"Crestview Elementary," Rocky yelled. "The last time we played them, their point guard ran to the bench crying because he could not do anything against us. Remember that, Coach Sully?"

"Yeah, I remember, and I bet his coach remembers as well. We'll have to think of something new to throw at him to freak him out again next week. It's the last game of the season, and I want to go out with a bang. I want a big win for the blue team. But a tie would be nice too," I said and smiled at Dustin.

"Young people need models, not critics."

—John Wooden

CHAPTER 15

Final Game

THE FINAL WEEK WAS MORE about preparation than game readiness. We had decided to give the boys an awards dinner and present them with individual trophies. I had reserved the pizza joint next door, and we were going to meet there as soon as the game was over. I had confirmed that all of the trophies had come in and they were assigned to the correct player. Honestly, I think I was more excited about this awards presentation than probably the kids were. Rocky's mother, Rachel, had just given birth to their second son (a future player for me) and was not going to make the dinner, so Dustin and I had to take care of all the arrangements. Fortunately for me, I had Tobie to help with setting everything up at the restaurant, or it may not have been done in time.

I scheduled an extra night of practice that week to get the boys some additional practice shooting the ball. The team worked really hard that week, and when I blew my whistle for the last time, I instructed the boys to huddle up in the center of the floor.

"I just wanted to let you boys know how proud I am of you guys. You have done really well this year. You worked very hard to become the team that every coach in our league is taking notice of. You have come so far from being a bunch of psychos running in circles out of control to a really good basketball team. I am sorry. A *great* basketball team. It has been an honor for me to coach you boys, and I will never forget you. I love you guys," I said as I stared into those sixteen eyeballs.

"Let's win this final game tomorrow for Coach Sully, who helped to get us here," Dustin added.

"Let's win for Coach Sully," several of the players echoed.

"Thank you, boys, very much. All hands in here. One final time. *Go, blue, on three. One, two, three.*"

"*Go, big blue!*"

The sound of their voices echoed off the old wood floor and brick walls like a cannon blast catching you unexpected at a high school football game. Not even a second after the words left their lips, they all tackled me in the middle of the floor. Of course this was prearranged by Dustin, but, nevertheless, there I was sprawled out on the floor laughing my butt off as a gang of seven-year-olds wrestled, pinched, punched, and tickled their old coach. Pete was right at home. I knew right then and there that this was what coaching was all about. This was what I was meant to do. I also realized lying there that several of these boys had reached that age where deodorant was desperately needed.

ON GAME DAY I WENT through all of the awards and who they were being presented to. I needed to make sure that I had everything correct. Once that was done, I worked up the game lineup. I had my starters selected and then proceeded with who was subbing for who and when. After enjoying my burnt eggs, burnt bacon, burnt toast, and burnt coffee, I headed out the door through the haze of smoke created by my weekly culinary masterpiece. I got in the truck and headed down that old two-lane road one final time en route to the gym.

We had the one o'clock game that day, and the parking lot was crowded. This usually was a good indication that the gym would be packed. As I entered the gym, I noticed several parents wearing their team colors and mascots on their T-shirts. There were a lot of cheerleading squads on the floor, including our own Wildcat cheerleaders, who I cannot remember ever seeing at a game of ours before that day. The concession stand was full of patrons in line waiting for their treats of cotton candy, hot dogs, nachos, and sodas. All of this was an indication of a pretty special day building up. You could just feel the excitement in the air. As I entered the gym through the typical double doors that had been greeting me for eight weeks, I noticed that the bleachers were packed with parents and friends on both sides of the court, here to see the next greatest coach masterfully call out his genius instruction to his team of basketball warriors, I thought to myself. The games had never been this crowded before. I guess it was the last game of the season for all the teams, which brought those out who each week kept promising they would come to see the next game, like I had a year before with Rocky. This definitely was going to be a thrilling day, and our team could not afford to let these people down.

As we took to the floor, I noticed the league director standing on the sideline talking to the official. This typically would not have caught my attention, but he was looking and gesturing in my direction as they were talking. After a couple of seconds, I shrugged it off and went back to working the team through their drills. Soon the horn went off, and the official signaled both teams to the center of the floor. I walked out on the floor with our team and helped assign who each player was guarding. I selected Reed to guard their point guard, who was the one who had run off the floor crying the last time we had played them. Their point guard looked up at me and said, "I don't want him guarding me."

"I don't care what you want," I said.

He then moved down the line out away from Reed and pointed to Kyle, who was standing across from him, and said, "I want him to guard me. He is a guard, and only a guard can defend a guard."

"Listen, I don't care where you walk to or who you stand in front of because I decide who defends who. Reed is guarding you today. I can have him guard you on the floor, on the bench, in the stands, and out to your car. He might even come over to your house just so he can guard you some more. Either way, it doesn't really matter what you want because he will be guarding you during this game today."

He ran over to his coach and complained, but there was nothing they could do. In basketball we do not get to choose who we want to guard us. I was never afforded that luxury, and neither would he. As long as Reed was playing in the game, he would guard their point guard.

The official tossed the ball in the air, and Crestview won the tip-off. They quickly came down and scored. We answered with a quick basket by Reed. The remainder of the quarter was tight, and when the horn went off, Crestview was up 4–3. During the time between quarters, Dustin and I reminded the team that this was their last game and that this was the game they would remember for the rest of their lives. "Are we playing this game the way we want to remember it?" we said to them.

The second quarter began with our team making the first two baskets, giving us the lead at 4–0. Crestview answered with their point guard scoring two baskets straight, tying the score at 4–4. So far we had not rattled their point guard to the point of tears, but there was still a lot of time left. The two teams battled, and midway through the quarter our team started pulling away from Crestview. Kyle and Ryan both scored a basket, and Reed hit a free-throw shot, giving us the lead at the end of the quarter, 9–5, and a halftime score of 12–9, blue team up.

By now our parents were really starting to make some noise in support of our team, and our section proved to be the loudest in the gym, which I always enjoyed. Both parents and cheerleaders were really cheering the boys on as they came walking off the floor for halftime. The sound of our fans and parents was deafening which caused both a feeling of admiration and appreciation inside of me. Although, it could have been my pregame hotdog instead.

I glanced down the sideline and noticed the director was talking to Crestview's coach. Again they were looking and pointing in my direction. I was starting to get annoyed with this distraction, and while the boys were going through their warm-up drills, I asked Dustin, "What do you think they are talking about?"

"I don't know, but he keeps looking this way. He was watching you the entire first half. What did you do to him?" Dustin asked.

"Nothing that I know of."

"Did you do or say anything to their coach?"

"Nothing other than good luck today."

"What about his son?" Dustin asked.

"His son? Who is his son?"

"Their point guard, you know, the one Reed is guarding."

"Well, that's just great. The boy who we made cry and storm off the floor in the last game against them turns out to be the son of our league's director."

"Yep, and the same kid you told before the game that you would have Reed guard him all the way home. It doesn't matter what we think they're discussing anyway," Dustin added.

"Why not?"

"Because you're about to find out; he's heading this way," he said as he walked off.

Before I could say a word to Dustin, the director approached me and said, "Coach Sully, do you have a second?"

"I suppose so. What's up?"

"I have some concerns about your team and the defense they play. They get an awful lot of fouls called on them."

"I don't know what you're talking about. They play very aggressively, but nobody on my team is intentionally trying to foul or hurt any other player."

"Try to clean it up," he said, totally ignoring what I had just said. "I counted nine fouls called on that Reed player of yours in just the second quarter."

"You mean that Reed player who happens to be guarding your son. Right?"

"Just try to clean it up before someone gets hurt out there, okay?" He smiled and walked to the other side of the floor.

You pompous son of a #!@!* I said to myself as he left the floor.

I huddled the kids together before the second half started and told them I wanted them to pull out all the stops on defense. I wanted to pressure them so hard that they would never want to play us again. No fouls, just pressure. They nodded in agreement. I also instructed Kyle to switch up which side he ran the offense to. I told him to rotate sides each time down the floor. I told them that we were going to run it down their little throats. Every time they missed a shot, we were to drive the ball all the way to the basket. I wanted to have the ball and our players down the floor before Crestview could get there. This is called a "fast break" or "run out," and the idea is to catch the other team not paying attention, loafing, or just not hustling to get back on defense. This was also the first time during the entire season that I allowed our team to run this. I wanted them to learn offensive plays first—learn how to set the offense up and to allow the entire team to get involved. Now, however, the brakes were definitely coming off. I was a little apprehensive at first because I wasn't sure how the team would respond. I didn't want this to turn into a chaotic mess. I was wrong. The boys exploded to start the second half.

We opened the third quarter with the ball and then a basket. We were off to a good start, and our fan section went absolutely crazy. After the first basket, we struggled with scoring again, but it wasn't due to our offense; it was due to the boys sprinting down the floor hard straight to the basket, causing them to get tired. Our defense was lethal, and it was just about two minutes into the half that their point guard threw a fit and was sent to the bench. As he walked to the bench, our parents applauded, making both him and his father even madder. I looked up in time to see his father and our director storm out of the gym. *So much for my coaching career*, I thought.

The quarter ended with our team up 4–2, and 16–9 for the game, with just one final quarter left to play for the season.

"Boys, this is it. You have to make it count. We're all very proud of you guys. Let's go out with a bang. Keep the pressure up, and run the ball nonstop. Don't worry about running our offense. Let's just run the ball, have fun, and beat them to the basket. Let's go one last time. Big blue, on three. One, two, three. *Go big blue!*"

With that, they took the floor and as soon as the ball was handed to Crestview, Kyle stole it and ran the floor for a score. That was an indication as to how this quarter was going to be played.

Then there was another steal and score by Ryan. Reed scored on a couple of fast breaks. The boys looked like seasoned ball players as they ran the floor, flawlessly converting knock-aways into steals and steals into points. Pete surprisingly and aggressively took the ball straight to the basket for two more points during one of our runs. Before you knew it, the quarter ended with the blue team up 10–2 for the quarter, which meant that we had won the game, 26–13.

The boys came running off the floor as if they had just wound down the final seconds of the NCAA championship basketball game and were about to become world champions. I was hugging Frank around the neck just in case he would lose it one last time. Then I squatted down to the floor as they came running over to jump on me in celebration. We had just finished the season with five wins, two losses, and one tie. This team, which did not have one win the previous year, had come so far. As we hugged and high-fived each other, I turned to see Dustin and Frank shaking hands and laughing. I looked up at the parents and gave a salute with a wink to several of them as they were applauding the boys. After several minutes of celebration on the sideline, we lined up to congratulate the other team as we customarily did after each game. I noticed after high-fiving each player just how out of breath their players were. We had completely beaten this team down to the point that they had absolutely nothing left. Their coach and I shook hands as I headed off the floor, up the bleachers, and over to the parents. We had an awards dinner to go to, and I wanted to get everyone moving in that direction. Besides, the last thing I needed was to have another meeting with the director, so I wanted to get out of Dodge as quickly as possible.

Loving the game

After several congratulations from the parents, I made my way toward the exit. As I approached the door, I stopped and turned around to take one last look at the playing floor, players, and parents. I wanted to inhale one last time the air of leather, sweat, and hardwood unadulterated by the aroma of cotton candy and hot dogs. I gazed upon every inch of the gym, bleachers, officials, and coaches. As I spanned the entire gymnasium, lost in the moment of reflection of one incredible season, my eyes stopped at my boys. They were not in any hurry to exit the building. They were not sitting watching the game being played before them. They were not bundled up holding on to their parents' hands preparing to exit into the bitter cold. They were still celebrating. Each one of them was laughing, slapping each other, and jumping up and down as if they were performing some tribal war dance. That's when it dawned on me. This one little brief moment in time, the boys were having the time of their lives, and that is what it's all about. I finally felt as if I had succeeded in doing the job I was asked to do.

As I continued standing there and gazing upon the celebration from our team, I realized that I wasn't simply staring at several young boys goofing off. I wasn't looking at several boys who made it through a transformation from raw, talentless children to the mighty basketball warriors who were standing in front of me. These kids came together through the season, becoming not a group of many components but instead a complete unit, each part relying on the other. They knew each other's strengths and fed off that. They became a team. They became a good team. They became the Great Eight, the greatest team to ever step onto the hardwood in the basketball-rich state of Kentucky.

CHAPTER 16

Awards Banquet and Final Good-Byes

THE RESTAURANT WHERE OUR BANQUET was to be held was right next door to the gym, so I arrived there very quickly and ahead of the players and parents. I searched the box that the trophies and awards were housed in, making sure that each of my players received one and that their names were on them next to the description of the award, such as "Best Offense, Best Defense," etc. There was one award in particular that I was looking forward to handing out the most. It was the Coach's Appreciation Award, and that was for Dustin. There was no possible way that I could have pulled this off without him. He was a big reason that we were successful, and I was very grateful to have him on our team.

It wasn't long before the place filled up with players, parents, and grandparents squeezing into a very small and cramped room. I was reviewing the notes that I had prepared when I noticed that a sense of nervousness was coming over me. I didn't understand this, since I had been addressing these same people for the past three months. I never had a fear of speaking in front of people, so it couldn't have been that. That's when I realized exactly what was going on. I knew this was it. This would be the last time that I would be addressing these boys, and I wasn't ready to say good-bye. I didn't want the season to be over, nor had I prepared myself for this very fact—this was the last time we all would be together.

The boys filled into the room and took their seats together at one large table. Dustin and I stood at the front of the room, and I had a table there for the trophies and awards. I cleared my throat, looked up at the now very overly crowded room, and began.

I gave my expression of gratitude to the boys, parents, grandparents, and friends. I then let those cramped inside that little room know just how much it meant to me to be the coach and mentor to these eight special boys. It was a heartfelt confession about how I never intended to get this drawn into coaching these boys and how I really was going to miss each of them. I explained how each boy was unique and offered his own special talent to the team, which is what made us so successful. I opened my heart, choking back tears at times, to convey to each and every one in attendance that these boys meant the world to me and coaching them was one of the greatest times I had ever had in my life. The room got completely quiet. You could have heard a pin drop in there. Then out of the quietness came the unmistakable sound of flatulence escaping from the boys' table. That is when pandemonium broke out. The boys fled the room, escaping what was sure to be a toxic gas filling the eyes and nostrils with a pungent odor. Given the fact that the room was so small, and we were all crammed inside there, the odor quickly filled the room, causing everyone to storm toward the door, trampling anyone in our way. And there I stood all alone just seconds after pouring my heart out, shaking my head. At that point the odor started overwhelming me, so I also made my way quickly out of the room with my hand over my mouth.

AFTER SEVERAL MINUTES, FRANK GAVE us the all-clear signal, and we started to refill the room, taking our original places. I took that opportunity to inform the boys that if that happened again, I would simply leave, taking the trophies with me. They knew I was serious, and the incident did not happen again, nor was it ever discussed. We proceeded with the awards presentation, and I started with the appreciation award.

"This award is for the person who tirelessly sacrificed a lot to help this team this year. He helped me in so many ways and certainly deserves more than this plaque. This year's appreciation award goes to ... Coach Dustin."

Dustin's jaw dropped. He approached me and shook my hand, and then, taking the award, he returned to his place in the room.

One by one the awards were handed out. After I announced the player the award was for, the boy would walk up to the front where I was standing. He would accept the trophy and then pose with me for a picture taken by the parents. This continued until all eight trophies were presented. What I found to be remarkable was that the boys guessed each recipient of every award before I announced it. It was a complete confirmation to both Dustin and me that we had it correct. To my surprise, at the end of the presentation, Dustin and I were each given coach jackets with our names embroidered on them, along with applause and thanks by the parents. I loved it. It was blue.

The boys were excited sitting at their table eating pizza, sharing their trophies with each other, and bragging about how they got their awards. I was just taking it all in, disappointed that this would be the last time we would all be able to spend time together. It wasn't just the boys I would miss; I had gotten to know the parents and some grandparents as well. This was our support, our cheering section, and chauffeurs to and from practices and games. I was fortunate to have the best group of people helping me with the team this year. After several minutes, I began packing up what I could. I glanced down at the sheet of paper that had the awards listed on it, displaying which player was getting what in order. It read:

Coach's Appreciation Award: Coach Dustin
Coach's Award: Brian Peterson
Mr. Hustle: Chad Nelson
Best Attitude: Wil Payne
Most Improved: Rocky Gaines
Best Sixth Man: Pete Self
Mr. Defense: Reed Messer
Mr. Intimidator: Ryan Nichols
Mr. Offense: Kyle Brentley

I did what I still do to this very day when I look at that sheet of paper and reflect on what was one remarkable season. I simply nod and smile. Who could have imagined that this bunch of basketball misfits would turn into one very competitive team? Who could have imagined that I would have let eight juveniles get to me like this group did? I never would have imagined that I would be sitting here writing a book about eight boys who put it all on the line for each other in order to have a season that they would never forget.

I mentioned earlier in this book that greatness comes in many forms these days, and there are a number of reasons I consider this team great. They overcame the fear of playing in front of spectators. They figured out how to play together even though in some cases throughout the season they did not really care for each other. They learned to trust each other and trust me as their coach—a complete stranger who they had never met before and neither had their parents. They listened to my instruction, trusting that what I had to say would benefit their game. Some of the boys were very small, weak, lacked athleticism, and had little if any experience. Yet, with all of these challenging differences in front of them, they found a way to come together to form a team.

A lot has happened since that awards banquet that dark and cold evening in the pizza place. The University of Kentucky won another NCAA championship title. I went on and coached another season with these boys. (Perhaps I will write another book about that team.) The University of Louisville won another NCAA championship title. I am getting ready to enter the boys into a spring and summer league, where they will be playing against some of the better teams in all of the tristate area. Regardless of what unfolds with this team from here on out, I will never forget that first season when 27.5, 8 feet 6, 4, and 8 became realized.

So in summary, just in case you missed it, 27.5 inches is the size of the ball with which youths play. It is much smaller than the typical basketball. Eight feet six is the height of the rim. The typical height for basketball is ten feet. Four was the quarters we played. We had to keep track of our game score because they started over each quarter with zero points. Eight. I bet you can figure this one out.

That was the number of players that I had to work with. Eight hard-working individuals. Yes, they were young and raw. Yes, they were difficult in the beginning to teach. Yes, they were at times hardheaded. But in the end, they really pulled together. They became a competitive, aggressive, and solid team.

They became the Great Eight, the greatest team that ever stepped onto the hardwood in the basketball-rich state of Kentucky.

Acknowledgments

I WOULD LIKE TO BEGIN with a thanks to Tobie for the support she gave me through what turned out to be a few different basketball seasons. I am grateful to her for her support and encouragement in both taking on coaching a team of second-graders and also for writing this book.

I would like to thank the following people who were instrumental in both my basketball development and in writing this book. First, I would like to acknowledge my brother, who through the years challenged me in games of one on one and horse on our neighbor's court. This, of course, afforded me the opportunity to become a much better player.

I certainly thank the parents of the kids who I coached. As much as I would love to introduce them to the readers, I decided not to release their names. Their parents were very instrumental in coaching this team; therefore, I greatly appreciate the trust and confidence they had put in me.

Meghan, my daughter, who gave me the first experience of developing someone's athletic skills for various sports. She would accompany me often to the football field for some Sunday flag ball and many evenings on the hardwood. We have a very special connection that still exists today.

My editors, who were able take my thoughts, which were jumbled on paper, and arrange them into the readable format that is this book.

Tobie's brother, Dustin, who convinced me to coach this team. By doing so, it allowed me the opportunity to experience greatness not found anywhere else. I am also very grateful for the assistance he gave me through the season. I could not have done this without him.

Dustin's wife and Rocky's mother, Rachel. She turned out to be as much a fan of the sport as I was and became a great person to bounce ideas off of. Her help and dedication to the boys was a tremendous load off my shoulders and was greatly appreciated.

Rocky. He was really the one who got me back into the great sport of basketball. His persistence in getting me to one of his games finally put me right back on the courts. His lack of skills forced me to take action in helping him to get better. This was what caused me to start coaching again. I guess you could say that if he wasn't so awful at the sport, I may have never experienced the Great Eight. Thank you, little buddy.

I would like to thank TJ and Bryan for allowing me the opportunity to coach this team and for the assistance they gave me throughout not only this season but the following season as well.

I would especially like to thank this team. They dedicated their time, sweat, and tears to become better players and a better team. Their hard work and dedication really chiseled them down into what we now know as the Great Eight.

I would like to thank you, the readers, for taking the time to read this book. There is no hidden agenda in writing this book, and I certainly never started this for any financial gain, but I always hope I could possibly reach those who would like to coach but for some reason do not. There is so much joy in teaching young boys and girls something that's new to them.

It's a tremendous feeling to see them finally get what you are instructing for the first time. You can actually see the light turn on in their little heads.

It's not easy by any means, and your patience will definitely be tried more than you could ever imagine, trust me. The joy you will receive, however, outweighs any negatives with which you might be concerned. Just do it. Volunteer at your child's school or approach a coach and offer your assistance. Believe me, it is much needed. You will never regret it.

And if you happen to be passing through Northeast Kentucky around basketball season, stop by one of the gyms and say hello. You will probably find me there with the old whistle in my mouth and the ball on my side, offering advice to some young ball player. What can I say? I am hooked, and you will be too.